The Eye of Argon
And the Further
Adventures of Grignr the
Barbarian

The Eye of Argon And the Further Adventures of Grignr the Barbarian

edited by
Michael A. Ventrella

Fantastic Books
1380 East 17 Street, Suite 2233
Brooklyn, New York 11230
www.FantasticBooks.biz

ISBN: 978-1-5154-4788-7

First Edition

Table of Contents

Foreword:

The Eye of Argon and Associated Earnest Musings
Jody Lynn Nye

Like the writers and re-enactors in the following digest, I, too, encountered "The Eye of Argon" at a science-fiction convention. I was invited to a private after-hours group, not quite sworn to secrecy, but cautioned that what I was about to behold was special, very funny, and well worth my time.

You can say that again. But I digress.

Like videotapes of the time, the manuscript that one of the grinning people in the room withdrew from her file bag had been copied many times, almost to the point of illegibility, and enjoyed a shamefaced existence, but lots of people wanted to have it. Michael A. Ventrella will describe to you the custom in which the manuscript was celebrated, and still is, although the secrecy surrounding it has finally ceased. And quite rightly, too.

Scholarly writings have been committed on "The Eye of Argon." You may think it's the last piece of literature deserving of any, but you'd be wrong. Many theses and dissertations have been written about works that have brought far less pleasure to readers than this, if not for the reason that the author himself would have wanted.

On my own part, I have used "The Eye of Argon" in my writers' workshops. We do the traditional rites, and it helps to assure my very nervous students that even if they are uncertain as to the quality of their writing, they'd have to go a long way to be as bad as this. Laughter breaks down a lot of barriers. It helps take the pressure off and allows even the most timid to open themselves to improvement. For this, Jim Theis, once a budding wannabe epic writer and now unwitting butt of many a snarky remark, I thank you.

Enjoy the following epic. Grignr awaits!

Jody Lynn Nye
August 2022

Introduction:

We Can All Be Grignr; or How to Appreciate Very Bad Writing

Michael A. Ventrella

So it's 1970. If you're a fan of high fantasy, you've read *The Lord of the Rings* and *The Hobbit*. There's no "Dungeons and Dragons," no high fantasy movies or TV shows, and now you're looking for something else.…

But all that's available is *Conan the Barbarian* and its clone, the *Gor* series.

Then again, you're a nerdy teenage boy with raging hormones, and fantasizing about being a strong hero who has beautiful women at his mercy is appealing.…

So put yourself back in those days and imagine young Jim Theis, who wants to be a writer. There are no home computers, no home printers, and photocopiers only exist in the largest corporations and cost tons of money. Even law firms and courthouses use carbon paper.

But there's also a mimeograph machine, where you type onto a certain specialized paper and feed it into a machine that can then print copies that are pale versions of the original. If you make a mistake typing, you either have to deal with it or rip the paper out of the typewriter and start all over. And that special paper isn't cheap.

You can even draw on the specialized paper, but you have to press hard and not make any mistakes. And forget about shading or color!

So Jim decides to write his own story. He has no training as a writer, has no patron to assist him, but he certainly has the enthusiasm required. He types away, ignoring mistakes, misusing words left and right, and having the time of his life, coming up with a story to impress his friends.

He then submits it to the Ozark Science Fiction Association, and they publish it in their little fanzine. Jim thinks that's the end of it—a nice little story some people will appreciate and then forget about.

However, the Forces of Fate have stepped in.

It falls into the hands of the science fiction community, which embrace it and start reading it for fun at parties, challenging each other to see how far they could get before breaking up laughing.

This extended to science fiction conventions, where a panel would try to get through it, and were required to read it as written, pronouncing the words exactly as they appeared while not laughing or screwing up.

Years pass as the story's distribution grows, shared from one convention to another. People all across America and Canada (and maybe elsewhere, too, who knows?) look forward to participating in the convention's reading sessions.

To add to the fun, the ending was missing. For some reason, the very last page had been lost, fallen from its stapley security, so no one quite knew how Grignr survived his final encounter. Theories abounded, and the search was on. Finally, according to Wikipedia, "a complete copy of the fanzine was discovered by special collections librarian Gene Bundy in the Jack Williamson Science Fiction Library at Eastern New Mexico

University in 2005." This was quickly distributed, and everyone lived happily ever after.

Well, except poor Jim Theis. He was unaware for quite some time of the notoriety his little story had generated, and had gone on to become a real writer, working as a journalist. He eventually learned people were gleefully reading and laughing at something he had written as a teenager. He was upset (as anyone would be). But he learned to live with it, and handled it well, knowing that if he objected over something he had done as a kid, he would come across as bitter. Instead, he shrugged and laughed along with everyone else.

Sadly, he died much too young, at age 48—but his story lives on, which is something all writers want.

And here's where I come in.

I had participated in the readings at various conventions over the years, but around 2006 or so (I can't remember the exact date), I was on a panel at Philcon, Philadelphia's science fiction convention, which, of course, takes place in New Jersey. I was the first reader, and even though I had done this before, I screwed up about three paragraphs in. That was it, I was removed from the panel. I got up to leave, and someone in the audience yelled, "Act it out!"

Being the ham I am, I readily agreed, and as the rest of the panel read, I pretended to be Grignr the Barbarian, wrestling giant rats, saving beautiful half-naked prisoners, and fighting evil clerics and nobles. The audience ate it up and laughed twice as hard as normal.

However, the person running the panel was not amused, and it was many years until I was once more invited to participate in the Eye of Argon reading at Philcon.

In the meantime, I had taken this to other conventions, and had organized a panel of writers who would read the story and act it out with me.

Part of the fun for us playing these roles at first was in not knowing what would come next. It was improv theater at its finest! But by doing this at various conventions in the northeast over the years, we got to the point where many of us knew the story by heart, and had various routines we would do that we knew would get laughs. Worse yet, if we tried reading, knowing the material, we hardly ever made mistakes or laughed.

So we evolved this into a game where we would invite the audience to participate, and once they were eliminated through reading, they were forced to act it out with us (to be replaced by the next audience member to read with us). Sometimes one of us would play Grignr, and sometimes we'd let the audience member have the starring role. The gender of the person playing Grignr or the half-naked femme fatale didn't matter, and, honestly, sometimes that just added to the hilarity.

I had a key group that was part of this almost every time, which included Keith R.A. DeCandido, Hildy Silverman, Gail Martin, and Ian Randal Strock—but many others were happy to play along, sometimes even willing to publicly humiliate themselves more than once. Among the ones I can remember are (in alphabetical order) Peter David, Ef Deal, Susan de Guardiola, Genevieve Eldredge, Charles Gannon, Marty Gear, C.J. Henderson, Walter Hunt, Daniel Kimmel, Tee Morris, Michael Pederson, Sarah Pinsker, KT Pinto, Peter

Prellwitz, Gray Rinehart, Ryk Spoor, Jean Marie Ward, and there's probably more I'm forgetting after all these years. Please forgive me if you're one of them and I left you off this list.

Some conventions specifically refused to allow the reading of the story, claiming we were making fun of someone who was no longer here and could not defend himself. Our reply was that he was aware of the readings when he was alive and did not ask that they be stopped, and come on, we all were terrible writers once. Okay, maybe not *that* bad, but hey, even Jim Theis became a professional writer eventually. Still, you won't find this being read at some conventions.

As this progressed, we also began showing the story on the screen so everyone could read along and see all the typos and mistakes. Ian Randal Strock annotated the story to show mistakes and corrections, and while this was a great way for everyone in the audience to appreciate the story better, we also found it was too distracting from the people actually performing the story. People would read along instead of watching the hams acting it out, and would miss a lot of funny bits.

We plan to continue to perform this, although we're all out of practice since many conventions were on hold for a few years due to the COVID virus. Still, we have plans to produce *Eye of Argon: The Play* in the future.

But all this led to an idea. What if we put Ian's annotations into a book form, and better yet, write some more stories in the same world? *The Further Adventures of Grignr the Barbarian!*

I contacted many of the people who had performed with us over the years and invited them all to submit a story. There were no requirements other than it needed to be funny. As we had no real budget to speak of, we promised each writer a grand total of $20 for their story. "This may be the only anthology I'll ever edit where a story may be rejected for being good," I said.

And some of the writers took me up on it. "I've just submitted the worst story I've ever written!" Keith bragged on social media. Jean got so excited she basically wrote a novelette. Dan took it off in different directions. Some made sure there were plenty of typos and misspelled words, and others decided the story itself was silly enough not to need them.

In any event, I hope you'll enjoy these tales and take them in the fun spirit in which they are intended. Mrifk!

Michael A. Ventrella
Summer 2022

Publisher's Apology
Ian Randal Strock

I'm almost ashamed to let this book go to press as is. One of the things on which I've prided myself while building Fantastic Books into a—I hope—well-respected publishing house is that our books are edited and proofread properly, and presented as close to letter-perfect as possible. Obviously, some typographical errors will always slip through, but I hope to keep them to an unnoticeable few.

After Michael presented me with the manuscript for this book, I read it as I always do, and tried to proofread it… and then I realized there was simply no way I could. Hildy's lead-off story, for example, is horrifying to me as an editor. It's a brilliant pastiche, not only misusing the same words Jim Theis did in the original "The Eye of Argon," but also replicating many of his actual misspellings and grammatical, punctuational, and typographical flubs. As an editor, it's painful for me to read; as a reader steeped in our shared history, it's incredible.

As I was "proofreading" the book, I gave serious consideration to pseudonymizing all the content, because you should know that every writer appearing in this book is far more accomplished and professional than these stories might lead one to believe. In the end, we decided that there will be no long-lost last page of this book: we stand up and proudly proclaim our minor parts in the ongoing legend of "The Eye of Argon."

So I hope you'll read this book with a proper sense of the love which produced it. Please know that we see all the errors you see (and probably some you might miss), and we have intentionally created them and let them be.

Ian Randal Strock (yes, really)
Brooklyn, New York
September 2022

The Eye of Argon
Jim Theis

"The Eye of Argon" first appeared in OSFAN #10 (November 1970), the publication of the Ozark Science Fiction Association. We present here resized scans of the original pages. Those pages were different colors; thus, the varying degrees of grayness in the backgrounds.

THE EYE OF ARGON

by Jim Theis

The weather beaten tamil wound ahead into the dust racked climes of the baren land which dominates large portions of the Norgolian empire. Age worn hoof prints smothered by the sifting sands of time shone dully against the dust splattered crust of earth. The tireless sun cast its parching rays of incandescence from overhead, half way through its daily revolution. Small rodents scampered about, occupying themselves in the daily accomplishments of their dismal lives. Dust sprayed over three heaving mounts in blinding clouds, while they bore the burdensome cargoes of their struggling overseers.

"Prepare to embrace your creators in the stygian haunts of hell, barbarian", gasped the first soldier.

"Only after you have kissed the fleeting stead of death, wretch" returned Grignr.

A sweeping blade of flashing steel riveted from the massive barbarians hide enameled shield as his rippling right arm thrust forth, sending a steel shod blade to the hilt into the soldiers vital organs. The disemboweled mercenary crumpled from his saddle and sank to the clouded sward, sprinkling the parched dust with crimson droplets of escaping life fluid.

The enthused barbarian swilveled about, his shock of fiery red hair tossing robustly in the humid air currents as he faced the attack of the defeated soldier's follow in arms.

"Damn you, barbarian" Shrieked the soldier as he observed his comrade in death.

A gleaming scimitar smote a heavy blow against the renegade's spiked helmet, bringing a heavy cloud over the Ecordian's misting brain. Shaking off the effects of the pounding blow to his head, Grignr brought down his scarlet streaked edge against the soldier's crudely forged hauberk, clanging harmlessly to the left side of his opponent. The soldier's stead whinnied as he directed the horse back from the driving blade of the barbarian. Grignr leashed his mount forward as the hoarsely piercing battle cry of his wilderness bred race resounded from his grinding lungs. A twirling blade bounced harmlessly from the mighty thief's buckler as his rolling right arm cleft upward, sending a foot of blinding steel ripping through the Simarian's exposed gullet. A gasping gurgle from the soldier's writhing mouth as he tumbled to the golden sand at his feet, and wormed agonizingly in his death bed.

Grignr's emerald green orbs glared lustfully at the wallowing soldier strugg-ling before his chestnut swirled mount. His scowling voice reverberated over the dying form in a tone of mocking mirth. "You city bred dogs should learn not to antagonize your better." Reining his weary mount ahead, grignr resumed his journey to the Norgolian city of Gorzam, hoping to discover wine, women, and adventure to boil the wild blood coursing through his savage veins.

PAGE 27

The trek to Gorzom was forced upon Grignr when the soldiers of Crin were loosed upon him by a faithless concubine he had wronged. His scandalous activities throughout the Simarian city had unleashed throngs of havoc and uproar among it's refined patricians, leading them to tack a heavy reward over his head. He had barely managed to escape through the back entrance of the inn he had been guzzling in, as a squad of soldiers bounced upon him. After spilling a spout of blood from the leader of the mercenaries as he dismembered one of the officer's arms, he retreated to his mount to make his way towards Gorzom, rumoured to contain hoards of plunder, and many young wenches for any man who has the backbone to wrest them away.

-2-

Arriving after dusk in Gorzom, grignr descended down a dismal alley, reining his horse before a beaten tavern. The redhaired giant strode into the dimly lit hostelry reeking of foul odors, and cheap wine. The air was heavy with choking fumes spewing from smoldering torches encased within thoden's earthen packed walls. Tables were clustered with groups of drunken thieves, and cutthroats, tossing dice, or making love to willing prostitutes.

Eyeing a slender female crouched alone at a nearby bench, Grignr advanced wishing to wholesomely occupy his time. The flickering torches cast weird shafts of luminescence dancing over the half naked harlot of his choice, her stringy orchid twines of hair swaying gracefully over the lithe opaque nose, as she raised a half drained mug to her pale red lips.

Glancing upward, the alluring complexion noted the stalwart giant as he rapidly approached. A faint glimmer sparked from the pair of deep blue ovals of the amorous female as she motioned toward Grignr, enticing him to join her. The barbarian seated himself upon a stool at the wenches side, exposing his body, na el save for a loin cloth brandishing a long steel broad sword, an iron spiraled battle helmet, and a thick leather sandals, to her unobstructed view.

" Thou hast need to occupy your time, barbarian",questioned the female?

"Only if something worth offering is within my reach." Stated Grignr,as his hands crept to embrace the tempting female, who welcomed them with o en willingness.

"From where do you come barbarian, and by what are you called?" Gasped the complying wench, as Grignr smothered her lips with the blazing touch of his flaming mouth.

The engrossed titan ignored the queries of the inquisitive female, pulling her towards him and crushing her sagging nipples to his yearning chest. Without struggle she gave in, winding her soft arms around the barshly bronzedhide of Grignr corded shoulder blades, as his calloused hands caressed her firm protruding busts.

"You make love well wench,"Admitted Grignr as he reached for the vessel of p potent wine his charge had been quaffing.

A flying foot caught the mug Grignr had taken hold of, sending its blood red contents sloshing over a flickering crescent; leashing tongues of light orange flame to the foot trodden floor.

PAGE 28

"Remove yourself Sirrah, the wench belongs to me" Blubbered a drunken soldier, too far consumed by the influences of his virile brew to take note of the superior size of his adversary.

Grignr lithly bounded from the startled female, his face lit up to an ashen red ferocity, and eyes locked in a searing feral blaze toward the swaying soldier.

"To hell with you , braggard!" Bellowed the angered Ecordian, as he hafted his finely honed broad sword.

The staggering soldier clumsily reached towards the pommel of his dangling sword, but before his hands ever touched the oaken hilt a silvered flash was slicing the heavy air. The thews of the savages lashing right arm bulged from the glistening bronzed hide as his blade bit deeply into the soldiers neck, loping off the confused head of his senseless tormentor.

With a nauseating thud the severed oval toppled to the floor, as the segregated torso of Grignr's bovine antagonist swayed, then collapsed in a pool of swirled crimson.

In the confusion the soldier's fellows confronted Grignr with unsheathed cutlasses, directed toward the latters scowling make-up.

"The slut should have picked his quarry more carefully!" Soared the victor in a mocking baritone growl, as he wiped his dripping blade on the prostrate form, and returned it to its scabbard.

"The fool should have shown more prudence, however you shall rue your actions while rotting in the pits. Stated. one of the sprawled soldier's comrades.

Grignr's hand began to remove his blade from its leather housing, but retarted the motion in face of the blades waving before his face.

"Dismiss your hand from the hilt, barbarbian, or you shall find a foot of steel sheathed in your gizzard."

Grignr weighed his position observing his plight, where-upon he took the soldier's advice as the only logical choice. To attempt to hack his way from his pre-sent predicament could only warrant certain death. He was of no mind to bring upon his own demise if an alternate path presented itself. The will to necessitate his life forced him to yeild to the superior force in hopes of a moment of carlessness later upon the part of his captors in which he could effect a more plausible means of escape.

"You may steady your arms, I will go without a struggle."

"Your decision is a wise one, yet perhaps you would have been better off had you forced death," the soldier's mouth wrinkled to a sadistic grin of knowing mirth as he prodded his prisoner on with his sword point.

After an indiscriminate period of marching through slinking alleyways and dim moonlighted streets the procession confronted a massive metaglia. The palace area was surrounded by an iron grating, with a lush garden upon all sides.

The group was admitted through the gilded gateway and Grignr was lodalong a stone pathway bordered by plush vegitation lustfully enhanced by the moon's shimmering rays. Upon reaching the palace the group was granted entrance, and after several minutes of explanation, led through several winding corridors to a richly draped chamber.

Confronting the group was a short stocky man seated upon a golden throne. Tapestries of richly draped regal blue silk covered all walls of the chamber, while the steps leading to the throne were plated with sparkling white ivory. The man upon the throne had a naked wench seated at each of his arms, and a trusted advisor seated in back of him. At each corner of the chamber a guard stood at attention, with upraised pikes supported in their hands, golden chainmail adorning their torso's and barred helmets emitting scarlet plumes enshrouding their heads. The man rose from his throne to the dias surrounding it. His plush turquois robe dangled loosely from his chunky frame.

The soldiers surrounding Grignr fell to their knees with heads bowed to the stone masonry of the floor in fearful dignity to their sovereign, leige.

"Explain the purpose of this intrusion upon my chateaul"

"Your sironity, resplendent in noble grandeur, we have brought this yokel before you (the soldier gestured toward Grignr) for the redress or your all knowing wisdom in judgement regarding his fate."

"Down on your knees, lout, and pay proper homage to your sovereign!" commanded the pudgy noble of Grignr.

"By the surly beard of Hrifk, Grignr kneels to no man!" scowled the massive barbarian.

"You dare to deal this blasphemous act to me! You are indeed brave stranger, yet your valor smacks of foolishness."

"I find you to be the only fool, sitting upon your pompous throne, enhancing the rolling flabs of your belly in the midst of your elaborate luxuryand . . ." The soldier standing at Grignr's side smote him heavily in the face with the flat of his sword, cutting short the harsh words and knocking his battered helmet to the masonry with an echo-ing clang.

The paunchy noble's sagging round face flushed suddenly pale, then pastily lit up to a lustrous cherry red radiance. His lips trembled with malicious rage, while emitting a muffled sibilant gibberish. His sagging flabs rolled like a tub of upset jelly, then compressed as he sucked in his gut in an attempt to conceal his softness.

PAGE 30

The prince regained his stature, then spoke to the soldiers surrounding Grignr, his face conforming to an ugly expression of sadistic humor.

"Take this uncouth heathen to the vault of misery, and be sure that his agonies are long and drawn out before death can release him."

"As you wish sire, your command shall be heeded immediately," answered the soldier on the right of Grignr as he stared into the barbarians seemingly unaffected face.

The advisor seated in the back of the noble slowly rose and advanced to the side of his master, motioning the wenches seated at his sides to remove themselves. He lowered his head and whispered to the noble.

"Eminence, the punishment you have decreed will cause much misery to this scum, yet it will last only a short time, then release him to a land beyond the sufferings of the human body. Why not mellow him in one of the subterranean vaults for a few days, then send him to life labor in one of your burial mines. To one such as he, a life spent in the confinement of the stygian pits will be an infinitely more appropriate and lasting torture."

The noble cupped his drooping double chin in the folds of his brining palm, meditating for a moment upon the rationality of the councilor's word's, then raised his shaggy brown eyebrows and turned towards the advisor, eyes aglow.

". . .As always Agafnd, you speak with great wisdom. Your words ring of great knowledge concerning the nature of one such as he ," sayeth , the king. The noble turned towards the prisoner with a noticable shimmer reflecting in his frog-like eyes, and his lips contorting to a greasy grin. "I have decided to void my previous decree. The prisoner shall be removed to one of the palaces underground vaults. There he shall stay until I have decided that he has sufficiently simmered, whereupon he is to be allowed to spend the remainder of his days at labor in one of my mines."

Upon hearing this, Grignr realized that his fate would be far less merciful than death to one such as he, who is used to roaming the countryside at will. A life of confinement would be more than his body and mind could stand up to. This type of life would be immeasurably worse than death.

"I shall never understand the ways if your twisted civilization. I simply defend my honor and am condemned to life confinement, by a pig who sits on his royal ass wooing whores, and knows nothing of the affairs of the land he imagines to rule!" Lectures Grignr ?

"Enough of this! Away with the slut before I loose my control!"

Seeing the peril of his position, Grignr searched for an opening. Crushing prudence to the sward, he plowed into the soldier at his left arm taking hold of his sword, and bounding to the dias supporting the prince before the startled guards could regain their composure. Agafnd leaped Grignr and his sire, but found a sword blade permeating the length of his ribs before he could loosed his weapon.

PAGE 31

The councilor slumped to his knees as Grignr slid his crimsoned blade from Agfnd's rib cage. The fat prince stood undulating in insurmountable fear before the edge of the fiery sanal comet, his flabs of jellied blubber pulsating to and fro in ripples of flowing terror.

"Where is your wisdom and power now, your majesty?" Growled Grignr.

The prince went rigid as Grignr discerned him glaring over his shoulder. He smiled to note the cause of the noble's attention, raised his sword over his head, and prepared to lensh a vicious downward cleft, but fell short as the haft of a steel rimed pike clashed against his unguarded skull. Then blackness and solitude. Silence enshrouding and ever peaceful mind supreme.

"Before me, sirrah! Before me as always: Ha, Ha Ha, Haaaa . . . " nobly cackled.

-2-

Consciousness returned to Grignr in stygmatic pools as his mind gradually cleared of the cobwebs cluttering its inner recesses, yet the stygian cloud of char -coal ebony remained. An incompatible shield of blackness, enhanced by the blank abscense of sound.

Grignr's muddled brain reeled from the shock of the blow he had recieved to the base of his skull. The events leading to his predicament were slow to filter back to him. He dickered with the notion that he was dead and had descended or sunk, however it may be, to the shadowed land beyond the the aparature of the grave, but rejected this hypothesis when his memory sifted back within his grips. This was not the land of the dead, it was something infinitely more precarious than anything the grave could offer. Death promised an infinity of peace, not the finit, misery of an inactive life of confined torture, forever concealed from the life bearing shafts of the beloved rising sun. The orb that had been before taken for granted, yet now cherished above all else. To be forever refused further glimpses of the snow capped summits of the land of his birth, never again to witness the thrill of plundering unexplored lands beyond the crest of a bleeding horizon, and perhaps worst of all the denial to ever again encompass the lustful excitement of caressing the naked curves of the body of a trim young wench.

This was indeed one of the buried chasms of Hell concealed within the inner depths of the palaces deeptzed interior. A fearful ebony chamber devised to drive to the brinks of insanity the minds of the unfortunately condemned, through the inept solitude of a limbo of listless dreary silence.

-3½-

A tightly rung elliptical circle of torches cast their wavering shafts prancing morbidly over the smooth surfaces of a rectangular, ridged altar. Expertly chisled forms of grotesque gargoyles graced the oblique rim protruberating the length of the grim orifice of death, staring forever ahead into nothingness in complete ignorance of the bloody rites enacted in their presences. Brown flaking stains decorated the golden surface of the ridge surrounding the altar, which banked to a small slit at the lower right hand corner of the altar. The slit stood above a crudely pounded pail which had several silver meshed chalices hanging at its sides. Dangling at the rim of golden mallet, the handle of which was engraved with images of twisted faces and grooved at its far end with slots designed for a snug hand grip. The head of the mallet was slightly larger than a clenched fist and shaped into a smooth oval mass.

Encircling the marble altar was a congregation of leering shamen. Eerie chants of a bygone age, originating unknown eons before the memory of man, were being uttered from the burial recesses of the acolytes' deep lings. Orange paint was smeared in generous globules over the tops of the Priests' wrinkled shaven scalps, while golden rings projected from the lobes of their pink ears. Ornate robes of luscious purple satin enclosed their bulging torsos, attached around their waists with silvered silk lashes latched with ebony buckles in the shape of moross mis-shaped skulls. Dangling around their necks were oval fashoned medalions held by thin gold chains, featuring in their centers blood red rubys which resembled crimson fatish eyeballs. Cushioning their bare feet were plush red felt slippers with pointed golden spikes projecting from their tips.

Situated in front of the altar, and directly adjacent to the copper pail was a massive jade idol; a misshaped, hideous bust of the shamens' pagan diety. The shimmering green idol was placed in a sitting posture on an ornately curved golden throne raised upon a round, ivory plated disc; it bulging arms and webbed hands resting on the padded arms of the seat. Its head was entwined in golden snake-like coils hanging over its oblong ears, which tappered off to thin hollow points. Its nose was a bulging triangular mass, sunken in at its sides with low gaping nostrils. Dramatic beneath the nostrils was a twisted, shaggy lipped mouth, giving the impression of a slovering sadistic grimace.

At the foot of the heathen diety a slender, pale faced female, naked but for a golden, jeweled harness enshrouding her huge outcropping breasts, supporting long silver laces which extended to her thigh, stood before the pearl white field with noticeable shivers traveling up and down the length of her exquisitely molded body. Her delicate lips trembled beneath soft narrow hands as she attemped to conceal herself from the piercing stare of the ambivalent idol.

Glaring directly down towards her was the stoney, myeloptic face of the bloated diety. Gaping from its single obling socket was scintillating, many faceted scarlet emerald, a brilliant gem seeming to possess a life all of its own. A priceless gleaming stone, capable of domineering the wealth of conquering empires... the eye of Argon.

- 4 -

All knowledge of measuring time had escaped Grignr. When a person is deprived of the sun, moon, and stars, he looses all conception of time as he had previously understood it. It seemed as if years had passed if time was being measured by terms of misery and mental anguish, yet he estimated that his stay had only been a few days in length. He has slept three times and had been fed five times since his awakening in the crypt. However, when the motions of a body are restricted its needs are also affected. The need for nourish ment and slumber are directly proportional to the functions the body has performed, meaning that when free and active Grignr may become hungry every six hours and witness the desire for sleep every fifteen hours, whereas in his present condition he may encounter the need for food every ten hours , and the want for rest every twenty hours. All methods he had before depended u on were extinct in the dismal pit. Hence, he may have been imprisoned for ten minutes or ten years, he did not know, resulting in a disheartened emotion deep within his being.

The food, if you can honor the moldering lumps of fetid mush to that extent, was born to him by two guards who opened a portal at the top of his enclos- ure and shoved it to him in wooden bowls, retrieving the food and water bowls from his previous meal at the same time, after which they threw back the bolts on the ironlatch and returned to their other duties. Since deprived of all other means of nourishment, Grignr was impelled to eat the tainted slop in order to ward off the pangs of starvation, though as he stuffed it into his mouth with his filthy fingers and struggled to force it down his throat, he imagined it was that which had been spurned by the hounds stationed at various segments of the palace.

There was little in the barem vault that could occupy his body or mind. He had paced out the length and width of the enclosure time and time again and tested every granite slab which consisted the walls of the prison in hopes of find- ing a hidden passage to freedom, all of which was to no avail other than to keep him busy and distract his mind from wandering to thoughts of what he believed was his future. He had memorized the number of strides from one end to the other of the cell, and knew the exact number of slabs which made up the black dungeon. Numerous schemes were introduced and alternately discarded in turn as they succored to unravel to him no means of escape which stood the slightest chance of sucess.

Anguish continued to mount as his means of occupation were rapidly exhaus t- ed. Suddenly without no tive, he wasrouted from his contemplations as he detected a faint scratching sound at the end of the crypt opposite him. The sound seemed to be causedly something trying to scrape away at the granite blocks the floor of the enclosure consisted of, the sandy scratching of something like an animl's claws.

Grignr gradually groped his way to the other end of the vault carefully feeling his way along with his hands ahead of him. When a few inches from the wall, a loud, penetrating squeal, and the scampering of small padded feet reverberated from the walls of the roughly hewn chamber.

Grignr threw his hands up to shield his face, and flung himself backwards upon his buttocks. A fuzzy form bounded to his hairy chest, burying its talons in his flesh while gnashing towards his throat with its grinding white teeth;its sour , fetid breath scorching the spiraung barbarians dilating nostrils. Grignr grappled with the lashing flexor muscles of the repugnant body of a gargauuan brownhided rat, striving to hold its razor teeth from his juicy jugular, as its beady gray organne of sight glazed into the flaring emeralds of its prey.

PAGE 34

Taking hold of the rodent around its lean, growling stomach with both hands Grignr pried it from his crimson rent breast, removing small patches of flayed flesh from his chest in the motion between the squalid dusk claws of the starving beast. Holding the rodent at arms length, he cupped his righthand over its frothing face, contracting his fingers into a vice-like fist over the quivering head. Retraining his grips on the rat, grignr flexed his outstretched arms while slowly twisting his right hand clockwise and his left hand counter clockwise motion. The rodent let out a tortured squall, drawing scarlet as it violently dug its foam flecked fangs into the barbarians sweating palm, causing his face to contort to an ugly grimace as he cursed beneath his breath.

With a loud crack the rodents head parted from its squirming torso, semi-ing out a sprinkling shower of crimson gore, and trailing a slimy string of disjoint-ed vurtulras, snapped trachea, esophagus, and jugular, disjointed hyoid bone, across purpled stretched hide, and blood seared muscles.

Flinging the broken body to the floor, Grignr shook his blood streaked hands and wiped them against him thigh until dry, then wiped the blood that had show-ered his face and from his eyes. Again sitting himself upon the jagged floor, he prepared to once more revamp his glum meditations. He told himself that as long as he still breathed the gust of life through his lungs, hope was not lost; he told him-self this, but found it hard to comprehend in his gloomy surroundings. Yet he was still alive, his bulging sinews at their peak of marvel, his struggling mind float-ing in a mirol of impressed excellence of thought. Plot after plot sifted through his mind in energetic contemplations.

Then it hit him. Minutes may have passed in silent thought or days, he could not tell, but he stumbled at last upon a plan that he considered as holding a slight margin of plausibility. He might die in the attempt, but he knew he would not submit without a final bloody struggle. It was not a foolproof plan, yet it built up a store of renewal vortexed energy in his overwroughtsoul, though he might perish in the execution of the escape, he would still be escaping the life of infinite torture in store forhim. Either way he would still cheat the gloating prince of the succored revenge his sadistic mind craved so dearly.

The guards would soon come to bear him off to the prince's burial mines of dread, giving him the sought after opportunity to execute his newly formulated plan. Groping his way along the rough floor Grignr finally found his tool in a pool of congealed gore; the carcass of the decapitated rodent; the tool that the very filth he had been sentenced too, spawned. When the time came for action he would have to be prepared, so he set himself to rending the sticky hulk in grim silence, search-ing by the touch of his fingertips for the lever to freedom.

-5-

"Up to the altar and be done with it wench;" ordered a fidgeting shaman as he gave the female a grim stare accompanied by the wrinkling of his lips to a mirth-ful grin of delight.

PAGE 35

The girl burst into a slow steady whisper, stooping shakily to her knees and cringing woefully from the priest with both arms wound snake-like around the bulging jade jade shin rising before her scantily attired figure. Her face was really inflamed from the salty flow of tears spouting from her glassy dilated eyeballs.

With short, heavy footfalls the priest approached the female, his piercing stare never wavering from her quivering young countenance. Halting before the terrified girl he projected his arm outward and motioned her to arise with an upward movement of his hand. the girl's whimpering increased slightly and she sunk closer to the floor rather than arising. The flickering torches outlined her trim build with a weird ornate glow as it cast a ghostly shadow dancing in horrid waves of splendor over smoothly worn whiteness of the marble hewn altar.

The shaman's lips curled back farther, exposing a set of blackened, decaying molars which transformed his slovenly grin into a wide greasy arc of sadistic mirth and alternately interposed into the female a strong sensation of stomach curdling nausea. "Have it as you will female" gloated the enhanced priest as he bent over at his waist, projecting his ape-like arms forward, and clasped the female's slender arms with his hairy round fists. With an inward surge of his biceps he harshly jerked the trembling girl to her feet and smothered her salty wet cheeks with the moldy touch of his decrepid, dull red lips.

The vile stench of the Shaman's hot fetid breath over came the nauseated female with a deep soul searing sickness, causing her to wrench her head backwards and resurgitate a slimy, orange-white stream of swelling gore over the richly woven purple robe of the enthused acolyte.

The priest's lips trembled with a malicious rage as he removed his callous paws from the girl's arms and replaced them with tightly around her undulating neck, shaking her violently to and fro.

The girl gasped a tortured groan from her clamped lungs, her sea blue eyes bulging forth from damp sockets. Cocking her right foot backwards, she lashed it desperately outwards with the strength of a demon possessed, lodging her sandled foot squarely between the shaman's testicles.

The startled priest released his crushing grip, crimping his body over at the waist overlooking his recessed belly, wide open in a deep chasm. His face flushed to a rose red shade of crimson, eyelids fluttering wide with eyeballs protruding blindly outwards from their sockets to their outmost perimeters, while his lips quivered wildly about allowing an agonized wallow to gust forth as his breath billowed from burning lungs. His hands reached out clutching his urinary gland as his knees wobbled rapidly about for a few seconds then buckled, causing the ruptured shaman to collapse in an egg huddled mass to the granite pavement, rolling helplessly about in his agony.

The pathetic screeches of the shaman groveling in dejected misery upon the hand hewn granite laid pavement, worn smooth by countless hours of arduous sweat and toil, a welter of labor oozing through his clenched hands, attracted the perturbed attention of his comrades from their foetid ablutions. The actions of this this rebellious wench bespoke the creedence of an unheard of sacrilige. Never before in a

PAGE 36

lost maze of untold eons had a chosen one dared to demonstrate such blasphemy in the face of the cult's idolic diety.

The girl cowered in unreasoning terror, helpless in the face of the emblazoned acolytes' rage; her orchid tusseled face smothered betwixt her bulging bosom as she shut her curled lashes tightly hoping to open them and find herself awakening from a morbid nightmare. yet the hand of destiny decreed her no such mercy, the antagonised pack of leering shaman converging tensely upon her prostrate form were entangled all too lividly in the grim web of reality.

Shuddering from the clamy touch of the shaman as they grappled with her supple form, hands wrenching at her slender arms and legs in all directions, her bare body being molested in the midst of a labyrinth of orange smudges, purpled satin, and mangled skulls, shadowed in an eerie crimson glow; her confused head reeled then closted in a mist of engrossing ebony as she lapsed beneath the protective shout of unconsciousness to a land peach and resign.

-6-

"Take hold of this rope," said the first soldier, "and climb out from your pit, slut. Your presence is requested in another far deeper hell hole."

Grignr slipped his right hand to his thigh, concealing a small opaque object beneath the folds of the g-string wrapped about his waist. Grins walls swelled in Grignr's cold, jade squinting eyes, which grown accustomed to the gloom of the stygian pools of ebony engulfing him, were bedazzled and blinded by flickerer -ing radiance cast forth by the second soldiers's resin torch.

Tightly gripped in the second soldier's right hand, opposite the intermittent torch, was a large double edged axe, a long leather wound oaken handled transfixing the center of the weapon's iron head. Adorning the torsoes of both of the sentries were thin yet sturdy hauberks, the breastplates of which we e woven of tightly hemmed twines of reinforced silver braiding. Cupping the soldiers' feet were thick leather sandals, wound about their shins to two inches below their knees. Wrapped about their waists were wide satin girdles, with slender bladed poniards dangling loosely from them, the hilts of which featured scarlet encrusted gems. Resting upon the manes of their heads, and reaching midway to their brows were smooth copper morions. Spiraling the lower portion of the helmet were short, upcurved silver spikes, while a golden hump spired from the top of each bas net. Beneath their chins, wound around their necks, and draping their clad shoulders dangled regal purple satin cloaks, which flowed midway to the soldiers feet.

hand over hand, feet braced against the dank walls of the enclosure, huge Grignr ascended from the moldering depths of the forlorn abyss. His swelled limbs, stiff due to the boredom of a aimless inactivity, compounded by the musty stagnature and jagged granite protuberan against his body, craved for action. The opportunity now presenting itself served the purpose of oiling his rusty joints, and honing his dulled senses.

PAGE 37

He braced himself, facing the second soldier. The sentry's stature was ·
was wildly exaggerated in the glare of the flickering cresset cuppex in his right
fist. His eyes were wide open in a slightly slanted owlish glaze, enhanced in their
sinister intensity by the hawk-bill curve of his nose andpale yellow pique of his
cheeks.

"Place your hands behind your back," said the second soldier as he raised
his axe over his right shoulder blade and cast it a wavering glance. "We must bind
your wrists to parry any attempts at escape. Be sure to make the knot a stout one,
Broig, we wouldn't want our guest to take leave of our guidance."

Broig grasped Grignr's left wrist and reached for the barbarians's right
wrist. Grignr wrenched his right arm free and .   .. swivoled to face Broig, reach-
beneath his loin cloth with his right hand. The sentry grappled at his girdle for
the sheathed dagger, but recoiled short of his intentions as Grignr's right arm
·   . . swept to his gorge. The soldier went limp, his bobbing eyes rolling beneath
fluttering eyelids, a deep welt across his spouting gullet. Without lingering to
observe the result of his efforts, Grignr dropped to his knees. The second soldier's
axe cleft over Grignr's head in a blaze of silvered ferocity, severing several
scarlet locks from his scalp. Coming to rest in his fellow's stomac , the iron head
crashed through mail and flesh with splintering force, spilling a pool of crimsoned
entrails over the granite paving.

Before the sentry could wrench his axe free from his comrade's carcass, he
found Grignr's massive hands clasped about his throat, choking the life from his
clamped lungs. With a zealous grunt, the Ecordian flexed his tightly corded biceps,
forcing the grim faced soldier to one knee. The sentry plunged his right fist into
Grignr's face, digging his grimy nails into the barbarians flesh. Ejaculating a
curse through rasping teeth, grignr surged the bulk of his weight forward,bowling
the besieged soldier over upon his back. The sentry's arms collapsed to his thigh,
shuddering convulsively; his bulging eyes staring blindly from a bloated ,cherry red
face.

Rising to his feet, Grignr shook the blood from his eyes, ruffling his
surly red mane as a brush fire swaying to the nightime breeze. Stooping over the spr
sprawled corpse of the first soldier, Grignr retrieved a small white object from a
pool of congealing gore. Snorting a gusty billow of mirth, he once more concealed th a
tiny object beneath his loin cloth; the tediously honed pelvis bone of the broken
rodent. Returning his attention towards the second soldier, Grignr turned to the
task of attiring his limbs. To move about freely through the dim recesses of the
castle would require the grotesque garb of its soldiery.

Utilizing the silence and stealth aquired in the untamed climbs of his
childhood, Grignr slink through twisting corridors, and winding stairways, lighting
his way with the confisticated torch of his dispatched guardian. Knowing where his
steps were leading to, Grignr meanders aimlessly in search of an exit from the
chateau's dim confines. The wild blood coarsing through his veins yearned for the
undafiled freedom of the livid wilderness lands.

PAGE 38

Coming upon a fork in the passage he trekked, voices accompanied by clinking footfalls discerned to his sensitive ears from the left corridor. Wishing to avoid contact, Grignr veered to the right passageway. If aquested as to the purpose of his presence, his barbarous accent would reveal his identity, being that his attire was not that of the castle's mercenary troops.

In grim silence Grignr treaded down the dingily lit corridor; a stalking panther creeping warily along on padded feet. After an interminable period of wandering through the dull corridors; he gaps to break the monotony of the cold gray walls, Grignr espied a small winding stairway. Descending the flight of arced granite slabs to their posterior, Grignr was confronted by a short hallway leading to a tall arched wooden doorway.

Halting before the teaming portal portal, Grignr rested his shaggy head sidewise against the barrier. Detecting no sounds from within, he grasped the looped metal handle of the door: his arms surging with a tremendous effort of bulging muscles, yet the door would not budge. Retrieving his axe from where he had sheathed it beneath his girdle, he hefted it in his mighty hands with an apiesed grunt, and wedging one of its blackened edges into the crack between the portal and its iron rimed sill. Bracing his sandaled right foot against the roughly hewn wall, teeth tightly clenched, Grignr applievered the oaken haft, employing it as a lever whereby to pry open the barrier. The leather wound hilt sending to its utmost limits of endurance, the massive portal swung open with a grating of snapped latch and rusty iron hinges.

Glancing about the dust swirled room in the gloomily dancing glare of his flickering cresset, Grignr eyed evidences of the enclosure being nothing more than a forgotten storeroom. Miscellaneous articles required for the maintenance of a castle were piled in disorganized heaps at infrequent intervals towards the wall opposite the barbarian's piercing stare. Utilising long, bounding strides, Grignr paced his way over to the mounds of supplies to discover if any articles of value were contained within their midst.

Detecting a faint clinking sound, Grignr sprawled to his left side with the speed of a striking cobra, landing harshly upon his back; torch and axe loudly clattering to the floor in a sourse of sparks and flame. A sharoven board leaped from collapsed flooring, clashing against the jagged flooring and spewing a shower of orange and yellow sparks over Grignr's startled face. Rising uneasily to his feet, the half stunned Ecordian glared down at the gruesome arm of death he had unwittingly sprung. "Imifki"

If not for his keen auditory organs and lightning steeled reflexes, Grignr would have been groping through the shadowed hell-pits of the Grim Reaper. He had unknowingly stumbled upon an ancient, long forgotten booty trap; a mistake which would have stunted the perusal of longevity of one less agile. A mechanism, similiar in type to that of a minature catapult was concealed beneath two collapsable sections of granite flooring. The arm of the device was four foot long, boasting razor like slants at regular intervals along its face with which it was to skewer the luckless body of its would be victim. Grignr had stepped upon a concealed catch which released a small metal latch beneath the two granite sections, causing them to fall inward, and thereby loose the spiked arm of death they precariously held in .

PAGE 39

Partially out of curiosity and partially out of an inordinate fear of becoming a pincushion for a possible second trap, Grignr plunged his torch into the exposed gap in the floor. The floor of a second chamber stood out seven feet below the glare. Tossing his torch through the aperture, Grignr grasped the side of an adjoining tile, dropping down.

Glancing about the room, Grignr discovered that he had descended into the palace's mausoleum. Rectangular stone crypts cluttered the floor at evenly placed intervals. The tops of the enclosures were plated with thick layers of virgin gold, while the sides were plated with white ivory; at one time sparkling, but now grown dingy through the passage of the rays of allencompassing mother time. Featured at the head of each sarcophagus in tarnished silver was an expugnisively carved likeness of its rotting inhabitant.

A dingy atmosphere pervaded the air of the chamber; which sealed in the enclosure for an unknown period had grown thick and stale. Intermingling with the curdled currents was the repugnant stench of slowly smoldering flesh, creeping ever slowly but surely through minute cracks in the numerous vaults. Due to the embalming of the bodies, their flesh decayed at a much slower rate than is normal, yet the nauseous odor was none the less repellant.

Towering over Grignr's head was the trap he released. The mechanism of the miniaturized catapult was cluttered with mildew and cobwebs. Notwithstanding these relics of antiquity, its efficiency remained unimpinged. To the right of the trap wound a short stairway through a recession in the ceiling; a concealed entrance leading to the mausoleum for which the catapult had obviously been erected as a silent, relentless guardian.

Climbing up the side of the device, Grignr set to the task of resetting its mechanism. In the a event that a search was organized, it wou'd prove well to leave no evidence of his presence open to wandering eyes. Besides, it might even serve to dwindle the size of an opposing force.

Descending from his perch, Grignr was startled by a faintly muffled scream of horrified desperation. His hair prickled yawdishly in disorganized clumps along his scalp. As a cold danced along the length of his spinal cord. No mortal/mortal barrier, human or otherwise, was capable of arousing the numbing sensation of fear inside of Grignr's smoldering soul. However, he was overwrought by the forces of the barbarians' instinctive fear of the supernatural. His mighty thews had always served to adequately conquer any tangible foe., but the intangible was something distant and terrible. His horrifying

PAGE 40

tales passed by word of mouth over glimmering camp fires and skins of wine had more than once served the purpose of chilling the marrowed core of his sturdy limbed bones.

Yet, the scream contained a strangely human quality, unlike that which Grignr imagined would come from the lungs of a demon or spirit, making Grignr take short nervous strides advancing to the sarcophagus from which the sound was issuing. Clenching his teeth in an attempt to steel his jangled nerves, Grignr slid the engraved slab from the vault with a sharp rasp of grinding stone. Another long drawn cry of terror infested anguish met the barbarian, soaring like the shrill piping of a demented banshee; piercing the inner fibres of his superstitious brain with primitive dread dread and awe.

Stooping over to espy the tomb's contents, the glittering Ecordians nostrills were singed by the scorching aroma of a moldering corpse, long shut up and fermenting; the same putrid scent which permeated the entire chamber, though multiplied to a much more concentrated dosage. The shriveled, leathery packet of crumbling bones and dried flacking flesh offered no resistance, but remained in a fixed position of perpetual vigilance, watching over its dim abode from hollow gaping sockets.

The tortured crys were not coming from the tomb but from some hidden depth below ! Pulling the reaking corpse from its resting place, Grignr tossed it to the floor in a broken, mangled heap. Upon one side of the crypt's bottom was attached a series of tiny hinges while running parallel along the opposite side of a convex railing like protuberances; laid so as to appear as a part of the interior surface of the sarcophagus.

Raising the slab upon its bronze hinges, long removed from the gaze of human eyes, Grignr percieved a scene which caused his blood to smolder not unlike bubbling, molten lava. Directly below him a whimpering female lay stretched upon a smooth surfaced marble altar. A pack of grimy faced shamen clustered around her in a tight circular formation. Crouched over the girl was a tall, pottbellied priest; his face dominated by a disgusting, open mouthed grimace of sadistic glee. Suspended from the acolyte's clenched right hand was a carven oval faced mallet, which he waved menacingly over the girl's shadowed face; an incoherent gibberish flowing from his grinning, thick lipped mouth.

In the face of the amorphos, broad breasted female, stretched out alluringly before his gaping eyes; the universal whim of nature filing a plea of despair inside of his white hot soul; Grignr acted in the only manner he could perceive. Giving vent to a hoarse, throat rending battle cry, Grignr plunged into the midst of the startled shamen; torch simmering in his left hand andax twirling in his right hand.

A gaunt skull faced priest standing at the far side of the altar clutched desparately at his throat, coughing furiously in an attempt to catch his breath. Lurching helplessly to and fro, the acolyte pitched headlong against the gleaming base of a massive jade idol. Writhing agonisedly against the hideous image, foam

PAGE 41

flecking his chalk white lips, the priest struggled helplessly - - -the victim of an epileptic seizure.

Startled by the barbarians stunning appearance, the chronic fit of their fellow, and the fear that Grignr might be the avantgarde of a conquering force dedicated to the cause of destroying their degenerated cult, the assam momentarily lost their composure. Giving vent to heedless pandemonium, the priests fell easy prey to Grignr's sweeping arc of crimsonal death and maiming distruction.

The acolyte performing the sacrifice took a vicious blow to the stomach; hands clutching vitals and severed spinal cord as he sprawled over the altar. The dimer anized priests lurched and staggered with split skulls, dismembered limbs, and spewing entrails before the enraged Ecordian's relentless onslaught. The howles of the maimed and dying reverberated against the walls of the tiny chamber; a chorus of hell frought despair; as the granite floor ran red with blood. The entire chamber was encompassed in the heat of raw savage butchery as Grignr luxuriated in the grips of a primitive, beastly blood lust.

Presently all went silenet save for the ebbing groans of the sinking shaman and Grignr's heaving breath accompanied by several gusty curses. The well had run dry. No more lambs remained for the slaughter.

The rampaging stead of death having taken of Grignr for the moment, left the barbarian free to the exploitation of his other persuials. Towering over his head was the misshapen image of the cult's hideous diety - - - Argon. The fantastic size of the idol in consideration of its being of pure mule was enough to cause the senses of any man to stagger and reel, yet thus was not the case for the behemoth. he had paid only casual notice to this incredible fact, while riveting the whole of his attention upon the jewel protruding from the idol's sole socket; its masterfully cut faucets emitting blinding rays of hypnotizing beauty. After all, a man cannot slink from a heavily guarded palace while burdened down by the intense bulk of a squatting statue, providing of course that the idol can even be hefted, which in fact was beyond the reaches of Grignr's coarsing stamina. On the other hand, the jewel, gigantic as it was, would not present a hinderence of any mean concern.

"Help me ... please . . . I can make it well worth your while," pleaded a soft, anguish strewn voice wafting over Grignr's shoulders as he plucked the dull red emerald from its roots. Turning, Grignr faced the female that had lured him into this blood bath, but whom had become all but forgotten in the heat of the battle.

"You": ejaculated the Ecordian in a pleased tone. "I though that I had seen the last of you at the tavern, but verilly I was mistaken." Grignr advanced into the grips of the femle's entrancing stare, severing the golden chains that held her captive upon the altars highly polished face of ornamental limestone.

As Grignr lifted the girl from the altar, her arms wound dexterously about his neck; soft and smooth against his harsh exterior. "Art thou pleased that we have chanced to meet once again?" Grignr merely voiced an sighed grunt, returning the damsels embrace while he smothered her trim, delicate lips between the coarsing protrusions of his reeking maw.

PAGE 42

"Let us take leave of this retched chamber." Stated Grignr as he placed the female upon h r feet. She swooned a moment, causing Grignr to iver her support then regained her stance. "Art thou able to find your way through the accursed passages of this castle? Nrifki Every one of the corridors of this damned place are identical."

"Aye; I was at one time a slave of prince Agaphim. His clammy touch sent a sour swill through my belly, but my efforts reaped a harvest. I gained the pig's liking whereby he allowed me the freedom of the palace. It was through this means that I eventually managed escape of the palace . . . . it was a simple matter to seduce the sentry at the western gate. His trust found him with a dagger thrust his ribs," the wench stated whimsicomically.

"What were you doing at the tavern whence I discovered you?" asked Grignr as he lifted the female through the opening into the mausoleum.

"I had sought to lay low from the palace's guards as they conducted their search for me. The tavern was seldom frequented by the palace guards and my identity was unknown to the common soldiers. It was through the disturbance that you caused that the palace guards were attracted to the tavern. I was dragged away shortly after you were escorted to the palace."

"What are you called by female?"

"Carthena, daughter of Minkardos, Duke of Barwego, whose lands border along the northwestern fringes of Gorzom. I was paid as homage to Agaphim upon his thirty-eighth year," husked the femme !

"And I am called a barbarian!" Grunted Grignr in a disgusted tone !

"Aye! The ways of our civilisation are in many ways warped and distorted, but what is your calling," she queried , hustily?

"Grignr of Ecordia."

"Ah, I have heard vaguely of Ecordia. It is the hill country to the far east of the Noregolean Empire. I have also heard Agaphim curse your land more than once when his troops were routed in the unaccustomed mountains and gorges." Sayeth she.

"Aye. My people are not tarnished by petty luxuries and baubles. They remain fierce and unconquerable in their native climes." After reaching the hidden panel at the head of the stairway, Grignr was at a loss in regard to its operation. His fiercest heaves wore as pebbles against burnished armouri Carthena depressed a small symbol included within the elaborate design upon the panel whereopen it slowly slid into a cleft in the wall. "How did you come to be the victim of these crazed shamen?" Questoed Grignr as he escorted Carthena through the piles of rummage on the left side of the trap.

PAGE 43

"By Agaphim's orders I was thrust into a secluded cell to await his passing of sentence. By some means, the priests of Argon acquire a set of keys to the cell. They slew the guard placed over me and abducted me to the chamber in which you chanced to come upon the accasstic sacrifice. Their hell-spawned cult demands a sacrifice once every three moons upon its full journey through the heavens. They were startled by your unannounced appearance through the fear that you had been sent by Agaphim. The prince would surely have submitted them to the most ghastly of tortures if he had ever discovered their unfaithfulness to Sargon, his bastard disty. Many of the partakers of the ritual were high nobles and high trustees of the inner palace; Agaphim's pittiless wrath would have been unparalled."

"They have no more to fear of Agaphim now!" Bellowed Grignr in a deep mirthful tone; a gleeful smirk upon his face. "I have seen that they were delivered from his vengence."

Engrossed by Carthena's graceful stride and conversation Grignr failed to take note of the footfalls rapidly approaching behind him. As he swung aside the arched portal linking the chamber with the corridors beyond, a suddened, blood lusting screech reverberated from his ear drums. Seemingly utilizing the speed of thought, Grignr swiveled to face his unknown foe. With gaping eyes and widened jaws, Grignr raised his axe above his surly mein; but he was too late.

-7-

With wobbling knees and swimming head, the priest that had lapsed into an epileptic siezure rose unsteadily to his feet. While enacting his choking fit in writhing agony, the shaman was overlooked by Grignr. The barbarian had mistaken the siezure for the death throes of the acolyte, allowing the priest to avoid his stinging blade. The sight that met the priests inflamed eyes nearly served to sprawl him upon the floor once more. The sacrificial mat it grin, blood splattered silence all around him, broken only by the occasional yelps and howles of his mained and butchered fellows. Above his head rose the hideous idol, its empty socket holding the shaman's ifurbished infuriated gaze. His eyes turned to a stoney glaze with the realization of the pillage and blasphemy. Due to his high succeptibility following the siezure, the priest was transformed into a raving maniac bent soley upon reaking vengeance. With lips curled and quivering, a crust of foam dripping from them, the acolyte drew a long ,wicked looking jewel hilted scimitar from his silver girdle and fled through the aperature in the ceiling uttering a faintly perceptible ceremonial jibberish.

-7½-

A sweeping scimitar swung towards Grignr's head in a shadowed blur of motion. With Axe raised over his head, Grignr prepared to parry the blow, while gaping wideeyed in open mouthed perplexity. Suddenly a sharp snap resounded behind the frothing shaman. The scimitar, halfway through its fatal sweep, dropped from a quivering nerveless hand, clattering harmlessly to the stoneage. Cutting his screech short with a bubbling, red mouthed gurgle, the lacerated acolyte staggered under the pressure of the released spring-board. After a moment of hopeless struggling, the shaman buckled, sprawling face down in a widening pool of blod and entrails, his regal purple robe blending enhancingly with the swirling streams of crimson.

"Mrrf! I thought that I had killed the last of those dogs!" muttered Grignr in a half apathetic state.

"Nay Grignr. You doubtlessly grew careless while giving vent to your lusts. But let us not tarry any long lest we over tax the fates.The paths leading to freedom will soon be barred. The wretch's cryn must certainly have attracted unwanted attention," the wench mused.

"By what direction shall we pursue our flight? "

"Up that stair and down the corridor a short distance is the concealed entrance to a tunnel seldom used by others than the prince, and known to few others save the palace's royalty. It is used mainly by the prince when he wishes to take leave of the palace in secret. It is not always in the Prince's best interests to leave his chateau in public view. Even while under heavy guard he is often assaulted by hurtling stones and rotting fruits. The commoners have little love for him," lectured the nobleman.

"It is amazing that they would ever have left a pig like him become their ruler. I should imagine that his people would rise up and crucify him like the dog he is."

"Alas, Grignr, it is not as simple as all that. His soldiers are well paid by him. So long as he keeps their wages up they will carry out his damned wishes. The crude implements of the commonfolk would never stand up under an onslaught of forged blades and protective armor; they would be going to their own slaughter," stated Carthena to a confused, but angered Grignr as they topped the stairway.

"Yet how can they bear to live under such oppression? I would sooner die beneath the sword than live under such a dog's command." added Grignr as the pair stalked down the hall in the direction opposite that in which Grignr had come.

"But all men are not of the same mold that you were born of, they choose to live as they are so as to save their filthy necks from the chopping block." Returned Carthena in a disgusted tone as she cast an appleced glance towards the stalwart figure at her side whose left arm was wound dexterously about her slim waist; his slowly waning torch casting their images in intermingling wisps as it dangled from his left hand.

Presently Carthena came upon the panel, concealed amongst the other granite slabs and discernable only by the tunnel cut crescent above it. "As I push the crescent aside push the panel inwards." Carthena motioned to the panel she was referring to and twisted the crescent in a counterclockwise motion. Grignr braced his right shoulder against the walling, concentrating the force of his bulk against it. The slab gradually swung inward with a slight grating sound. Carthena stooped beneath Grignr's corded arms and crawled upon all fours into the nassage beyond. Grignr followed after easing the slab back into place.

Winding before the pair was a dark musty tunnel, exhibiting tangled spider webs from it ceiling to wall and an oozing, muckily slime running lazily upon its floor. Hanging from the chipped wall upon Grignr's right side was a half moldered corpse, its grey flocking arms held in place by rusted iron manacles. Carthena flinched back into Grignr's arms at sight of the leering eat in an ugly distorted grimance; staring horribly at her from hollow gaping sockets.

"This abode must also be used by Agaphim as a torture chamber. I wonder how many of his enemies have disappeared into these haunts never to be heard from again," pondered the hulking brute.

"Let me flee before we are also caught within Agaphim's ghastly clutches. The exit from this tunnel cannot be very far from here!" wail Carthena with a slight sob in her voice, as she sagged in Grignr's encompasing embrace.

"Aye; It will be best to be finished with this corridor as soon as it is possible, but why do you flinch from the sight of death so? swiftl You have seen such death this day without exhibiting such emotions." Exclaimed Grignr as he led out treading fora along the dingy confines.

"---The man hanging from the wall was Doyanta. He had committed the folly of showing affections for me in front of Agaphim --- he never meant any harm by his actions!" At this Carthena broke into a slow steady whispering, choking her voice with gasping sobs. "There was never anything between us yet Agaphim did this to him! The beast! May the demons of Hell's deepest haunts claw away at his wretched flesh for this peralliess act!" she prayed.

"I regret that you felt more for this fellow than you wish to let on ... but enough of this. We can talk of such matters after we are once more free to do so." With this Grignr lifted the grieved femela to her feet and strode onward down the corridor, supporting the bulk of her weight with his surging left arm.

Presently a dim light was perceptibly filtering into the tunnel, casting a dim reddish hue upon the moldy wall of the passage's grim confines. Carthena had gained her whispering and partially regained her composure. "The tunnel's end must be nearing. Rays of sunlight are beginning to seep into ..."

Grignr clamped his right hand over Carthena's mouth and with a slight struggle pulled her over to the shadows at the right hand wall of the path, while at the same time thrusting his torch beneath an overhanging stone to smother its flickering glow. "Be silent; I can hear footfalls approaching through the tunnel," growled Grignr in a hushed tone.

"All that you hear are the horses corralled at the far end of the tunnel. That is a further sign that we are nearing our goal." She stated

"All that you hear is less than I hear! I heard footsteps coming towards us. Silence yourself lest we may find out whom we are being brought into contact with. I doubt that any would have thought as yet of searching this passage for us. The advantage of surprise will be upon our side." Grignr warned.

arthena cast her eyes downward and ceased any
further pursuit towards conversation, an
irritating habit in which she had gained
an amazing . . . . . .
proficiency. Two figures came into the pairs
view, from around a turn in the tunnel. They
were clothed in rich luxuriant silks and rambling o
on in conversation while ignorant of their crouching foes waiting in an ambush ahead.

"...That barbarian dog is cringing beneath
the weight of the lash at this very moment sire. He
shall cause no more disturbance."

"Aye, and so it is with any who dare to
cross the path of Sargon's chosen one." said the 2nd
man.

"But the peasants are showing signs of growing unrest. They complain that
they cannot feet their families while burdened with your taxes."

"I shall teach those sluts the meaning of humility! Order an immediate
increase upon their taxes. They dare to question my sovereign authority, Ba-a, they
shall soon learn what true oppression can be . I will ... "

A shadowed bulk leapt from behind a jutting promontory as it brought down
a double edged axe with the speed of a striking thought. One of the nobles sagged
lifeless to the ground, skull split to the teeth.

Grignr gasped as he observed the bisected face set in its leering death
agonies. It was Agafnd! The dead mans comrade having recovered from his shock drew
a jewel encrusted dagger from beneath the folds of his robe and lunged toward the
barbarians back. Grignr spun at the sound from behind and smashed down his crimsoned
axe once more. His antagonist lunged howling to a stream of stagnant green water,
grasping a spouting stump that had once been a wrist. Grignr raised his axe over his
head and prepared to finish the incomplete job, but was deterred half way through his
lunge by a frenzied screech from behind.

Carthena leapt to the head of the writhing figure, plunging a smoldering
torch into the agonized face. The howls increased in their horrid intensity, stifled
by the sizzling of roasting flesh; then died down until the man was reduced to a
blubbering mass of squirming, insensate flesh.

Grignr advance to Carthena's side wincing slightly from the putrid aroma
of charred flesh that rose in a puff of thick white smog throughout the chamber.
Carthena reeled slightly, staring dazedly downward at her gruesome handywork. "I had
to do it . . . it was Agaphim . . . I had to," " she exclaimed!

PAGE 47

"Sargon should be more carful of his right hand men." Added Grignr, a smug grin upon his lips. "But to hell with Sargon for now, the stench is becoming bothersome to me." With that Grignr grasped Carthena around the waist leading her around the bend in the cave and into the open.

A ball of feral red was rising through the mists of the eastern horizon, disipating the slinking shadows of the night. A coral stood before the pair, enclosing two grazing mares. Grignr reached into a weighted down leather pouch dangling at his side and drew forth the scintillant red emerald he had obtained from the bloated idol. Raising it towards the sun he said, "We shall do well with bauble, eh!"

Carthena gasped at the gem gasping in a terrified manner "The eye of Argon, Oh! Kalla!" At this the gem gave off a blinding glow, then dribbled through Grignr's fingers in a slimy red ooze. Grignr stopped back, pushing Carthena behind him. The droplets of slime slowly converged into a pulsating jelly-like mass. A single opening transafixed the blob, forming into a leechlike maw.

Then the hideous transgressor of nature flowed towards Grignr, a trail of greenish slime lingering behind it. The single gap puckered repeatedly emitting a ghastly sucking sound.

Grignr spread his legs into a battle stance, steeling his quivering thews for a battle royal with a thing he knew not how to fight. Carthena wound her arms about her protectors neck, mumbling, "Kill it! Kill!" While her entire body trembled.

The thing was almost upon Grignr when he buried his axe into the gristly maw. It passed through the blob and clanged upon the ground. Grignr drew his axe back with a film of yellow-green slime clinging to the blade. The thing was seemingly unaffected. Then it started to aloose up his leg. The hairs upon his nape stood on end from the slimey feel of the things ugly, bulk. The Nautous sucking sound became louder, and Grignr felt the blood being drawn from his body. With each hiss of hideous pucker the thing increased in size.

Grignr shook his foot about madly in an attempt to dislodge the blob, but it clung like a leech, still feeding upon his rapidly draining life fluid. He grasped with his hands trying to rip it off, but only found his hands entangled in a sickly glue-like substance. The slimey thing continued its puckering ; now having grown the size of Grignr's leg from its vampiric feast.

Grignr began to reel and stagger under the blob, his chalk white face and faltering muscles attesting to the gigantic loss of blood. Carthena slipped from Grignr in a death-like faint, a sorrow chilling scream upon her red rubish lips. In final desperation Grignr grasped the smoldering torch upon the ground and plunged it into the rocking maw of the travestry. A shudder passed though the thing. Grignr felt the blackness closing upon his eyes, but held on with the last ebb of his rapidly waning vitality. He could feel its grip lessening as a hideous gurgling sound erupted from the writhing maw. The jelly like mass began to bubble like a vat of boiling tar as quivers passed up and down its entire form.

PAGE 48

With a sloshing plop the thing fell to the ground, evaporating in a thick scarlet cloud until it reatained its original size. It remained thus for a moment as the puckered maw took the shape of a protruding red eyeball, the pupil of which seemed to unravel before it the tale of creation. How a shapeless mass slithered from the quagmires of the stygmatic pool of time, only to degenerate into a leprosy of avaricious lust. In that fleeting moment the grim mystery of life was revealed before Grignr's ensnared gaze.

The eyeballs glare turned to a sudden plea of mercy, a plea for the whole of humanity. Then the blob began to quiver with violent convulsions; the eyeball shattered into a thousand tiny fragments and evaporated in a curling wisp of scarlet mist. The very ground below the thing began to vibrate and swallow it up with a belch.

The thing was gone forever. All that remained was a dark red blotch upon the face of the earth, blotching things up. Shaking his head, his shaggy mane to clear the jumbled fragments of his mind, Grignr tossed the limp female over his shoulder. Mounting one of the disgruntled mares, and leading the other; the weary, scarred barbarian trooted slowly off into the horizon to become a tiny pinpoint in a filtered filed of swirling blue mists. Leaving the Nobles, soldiers, and peasants to replace the missing monarch. Long leave the king !!!!

by Jim Theis

winner of the Jay T. Rikosh award for excellence!

"The Eye of Argon" by Jim Theis
Annotated by Ian Randal Strock

This transcript of the text is reproduced as faithfully as possible from the scan (including letters, punctuation marks, and lack of spacing). However, end-of-line (and in a few cases, beginning-of-line) hyphens which are properly placed between syllables are omitted here, as is random excess spacing between words. In the original, in addition to indenting each paragraph, there is a line space between each paragraph.

The weather beaten trail wound ahead into the dust racked climes of the baren land which dominates large portions of the Norgolian empire. Age worn hoof prints smothered by the sifting sands of time shone dully against the dust splattered crust of earth. The tireless sun cast its parching rays of incandescense from overhead, half way through its daily revolution. Small rodents scampered about, occupying themselves in the daily accomplishments of their dismal lives. Dust sprayed over three heaving mounts in blinding clouds, while they bore the burdonsome cargoes of their struggling overseers.

"Prepare to embrace your creators in the stygian haunts of hell, barbarian", gasped the first soldier.

"Only after you have kissed the fleeting stead of death, wretch!" returned Grignr.

A sweeping blade of flashing steel riveted from the massive barbarians hide enameled shield as his rippling right arm thrust forth, sending a steel shod blade to the

barren

incandescence

burdensome

barbarian," gasped
stead (n., obsolete) – a place or locality

barbarian's

hilt into the soldiers vital organs. The disemboweled mercenary crumpled from his saddle and sank to the clouded sward, sprinkling the parched dust with crimson droplets of escaping life fluid.

The enthused barbarian swiveled about, his shock of fiery red hair tossing robustly in the humid air currents as he faced the attack of the defeated soldier's fellow in arms.

"Damn you, barbarian" Shrieked the soldier as he observed his comrade in death.

A gleaming scimitar smote a heavy blow against the renegade's spiked helmet, bringing a heavy cloud over the Ecordian's misting brain. Shaking off the effects of the pounding blow to his head, Grignr brought down his scarlet streaked edge against the soldier's crudely forged hauberk, clanging harmlessly to the left side of his opponent. The soldier's stead whinnied as he directed the horse back from the driving blade of the barbarian. Grignr leashed his mount forward as the hoarsely piercing battle cry of his wilderness bred race resounded from his grinding lungs. A twirling blade bounced harmlessly from the mighty thief's buckler as his rolling right arm cleft upward, sending a foot of blinding steel ripping through the Simarian's exposed gullet. A gasping gurgle from the soldier's writhing mouth as he tumbled to the golden sand at his feet, and wormed agonizingly in his death bed.

Grignr's emerald green orbs glared lustfully at the wallowing soldier struggling before his chestnut swirled mount. His scowling voice reverberated over the dying form in a tone of mocking mirth. "You city bred dogs should learn not to antagonize your better." Reining his weary mount ahead, grignr resumed his journey to the

soldier's

sward (n.) – the grassy surface of land, turf

swiveled

barbarian," shrieked *[missing comma; lower case]*

misting?

hauberk (n.) – long mail shirt
steed

grinding?
buckler (n.) – a round shield

writhing?
death bed?
lustfully?
swirled?

*Simarian? People from
ancient Sumer were Sumerian,
and Conan was a Cimmerian.*

betters
Grignr *[capitalized]*

Noregolian city of Gorzam, hoping to discover wine, women, and adventure to boil the wild blood coarsing through his savage veins.

The trek to Gorzom was forced upon Grignr when the soldiers of Crin were leashed upon him by a faithless concubine he had wooed. His scandalous activities throughout the Simarian city had unleashed throngs of havoc and uproar among it's refined patricians, leading them to tack a heavy reward over his head.

He had barely managed to escape through the back entrance of the inn he had been guzzling in, as a squad of soldierd tounced upon him. After spilling a spout of blood from the leader of the mercenaries as he dismembered one of the officer's arms, he retreated to his mount to make his way towards Gorzom, rumoured to contain hoards of plunder, and many young wenches for any man who has the backbone to wrest them away.

-2-

Arriving after dusk in Gorzom,grignr descended down a dismal alley, reining his horse before a beaten tavern. The redhaired giant strode into the dimly lit hostelry reeking of foul odors, and cheap wine. The air was heavy with chocking fumes spewing from smolderingtorches encased within theden's earthen packed walls. Tables were clustered with groups of drunken thieves, and cutthroats, tossing dice, or making love to willing prostitutes.

Eyeing a slender female crouched alone at a nearby bench, Grignr advanced wishing to wholesomely occupy his time. The flickering torches cast weird shafts of

Norgolian *[see first page]*
coursing

Gorzam *[see previous paragraph]*
leashed?

its

soldiers
*dismembered (v.) – divide
   limb from limb*
Gorzam

*tounced? How about
"pounced upon him"
or "trounced him"?*

Gorzam, Grignr *[space after comma; capitalized]*

red-haired
foul odors and cheap wine *[unnecessary comma]*
choking   smoldering torches
the den's
drunken thieves and *[unnecessary comma]*
cutthroats tossing dice *[unnecessary comma]*

luminescence dancing over the half naked harlot of his choice, her stringy orchid twines of hair swaying gracefully over the lithe opaque nose, as she raised a half drained mug to her pale red lips.

Glancing upward, the alluring complexion noted the stalwart giant as he rapidly approached. A faint glimmer sparked from the pair of deep blue ovals of the amorous female as she motioned toward Grignr, enticing him to join her. The barbarian seated himself upon a stool at the wenches side, exposing his body, naked save for a loin cloth brandishing a long steel broad sword, an iron spiraled battle helmet, and a thick leather sandals, to her unobstructed view.

"Thou hast need to occupy your time, barbarian",questioned the female?

"Only if something worth offering is within my reach." Stated Grignr,as his hands crept to embrace the tempting female, who welcomed them with open willingness.

"From where do you come barbarian, and by what are you called?" Gasped the complying wench, as Grignr smothered her lips with the blazing touch of his flaming mouth.

The engrossed titan ignored the queries of the inquisitive female, pulling her towards him and crushing her sagging nipples to his yearning chest. Without struggle she gave in, winding her soft arms around the harshly bronzedhide of Grignr corded shoulder blades, as his calloused hands caressed her firm protruding busts.

"You make love well wench," Admitted Grignr as he reached for the vessel of potent wine his charge had been quaffing.

lithe (adj.) – pliant, limber

complexion (n.) – the color, texture, and appearance of the skin

opaque (adj.) – not allowing light to pass through

wench's

a sandal or sandals?

barbarian," asked

reach," stated Grignr, as

gasped

bronzed hide   Grignr's
busts is a collective: two breasts, one bust
wench," admitted

A flying foot caught the mug Grignr had taken hold of, sending its blood red contents sloshing over a flickering crescent; leashing tongues of bright orange flame to the foot trodden floor.

"Remove yourself Sirrah, the wench belongs to me;" Blabbered a drunken soldier, too far consumed by the influences of his virile brew to take note of the superior size of his adversary.

Grignr lithly bounded from the startled female, his face lit up to an ashen red ferocity, and eyes locked in a searing feral blaze toward the swaying soldier.

"To hell with you, braggard!" Bellowed the angered Ecordian, as he hefted his finely honed broad sword.

The staggering soldier clumsily reached towards the pommel of his dangling sword, but before his hands ever touched the oaken hilt a silvered flash was slicing the heavy air. The thews of the savages lashing right arm bulged from the glistening bronzed hide as his b;ade bit deeply into the soldiers neck, loping off the confused head of his senseless tormentor.

With a nauseating thud the severed oval toppled to the floor, as the segregated torso of Grignr's bovine antagonist swayed, then collapsed in a pool of swirled crimson.

In the confusion the soldier's fellows confronted Grignr with unsheathed cutlasses, directed toward the latters scowling make-up.

"The slut should have picked his quarry more carefully!" Roared the victor in a mocking baritone growl, as he wiped his dripping blade on the prostrate form, and returned it to its scabbard.

"Remove yourself, sirrah, the wench belongs to me,"
blabbered

lithely

bellowed

savage's
blade
solder's   lopping

latter's

roared

"The fool should have shown more prudence, however you shall rue your actions while rotting in the pits." Stated one of the sprawled soldier's comrades.

Grignr's hand began to remove his blade from its leather housing, but retarded the motion in face of the blades waving before his face.

"Dismiss your hand from the hilt, barbarbian, or you shall find a foot of steel sheathed in your gizzard."

Grignr weighed his position observing his plight, where-upon he took the soldier's advice as the only logical choice. To attempt to hack his way from his present predicament could only warrant certain death. He was of no mind to bring upon his own demise if an alternate path presented itself. The will to necessitate his life forced him to yield to the superior force in hopes of a moment of carlessness later upon the part of his captors in which he could effect a more plausible means of escape.

"You may steady your arms, I will go without a struggle."

"Your decision is a wise one, yet perhaps you would have been better off had you forced death," the soldier's mouth wrinkled to a sadistic grin of knowing mirth as he prodded his prisoner on with his sword point.

After an indiscriminate period of marching through slinking alleyways and dim moonlighted streets the procession confronted a massive seraglio. The palace area was surrounded by an iron grating, with a lush garden upon all sides.

The group was admitted through the gilded gateway and Grignr was ledalong a stone pathway bordered by plush vegitation lustfully enhanced by the moon's

pits," stated

in the face

barbarian

whereupon

carelessness

*seraglio (se-**ral**-yoh, n.) – the part of a Muslim house or palace in which the wives and concubines are secluded; harem*

led along
vegetation

shimmering rays. Upon reaching the palace the group was granted entrance, and after several minutes of explanation, led through several winding corridors to a richly draped chamber.

Confronting the group was a short stocky man seated upon a golden throne. Tapestries of richly draped regal blue silk covered all walls of the chamber, while the steps leading to the throne were plated with sparkling white ivory. The man upon the throne had a naked wench seated at each of his arms, and a trusted advisor seated in back of him. At each cornwr of the chamber a guard stood at attention, with upraised pikes supported in their hands, golden chainmail adorning their torso's and barred helmets emitting scarlet plumes enshrouding their heads. The man rose from his throne to the dias surrounding it. His plush turquois robe dangled loosely from his chuncky frame.

The soldiers surrounding Grignr fell to their knees with heads bowed to the stone masonry of the floor in fearful dignity to their sovereign, leige.

"Explain the purpose of this intrusion upon my chateau!"

"Your sirenity, resplendent in noble grandeur, we have brought this yokel before you (the soldier gestured toward Grignr) for the redress or your all knowing wisdon in judgement regarding his fate."

"Down on your knees, lout, and pay proper homage to your sovereign!" commanded the pudgy noble of Grignr.

"By the surly beard of Mrifk, Grignr kneels to no man!" scowled the massive barbarian.

"You dare to deal this blasphemous act to me! You are indeed brave stranger, yet your valor smacks of foolishness."

upon a

corner

torsos

dais
turquoise

sovereign (n.) – a monarch　　*liege (n.) – a feudal lord*

Serenity
before you," the soldier gestured toward Grignr, "for the
redress of your

"I find you to be the only fool, sitting upon your pompous throne, enhancing the rolling flabs of your belly in the midst of your elaborate luxuryand ..." The soldier standing at Grignr's side smote him heavily in the face with the flat of his sword, cutting short the harsh words and knocking his battered helmet to the masonry with an echo-ing clang.

The paunchy noble's sagging round face flushed suddenly pale, then pastily lit up to a lustrous cherry red radiance. His lips trembled with malicious rage, while emitting a muffled sibilant gibberish. His sagging flabs rolled like a tub of upset jelly, then compressed as he sucked in his gut in an attempt to conceal his softness.

The prince regained his statue, then spoke to the soldiers surrounding Grignr, his face conforming to an ugly expression of sadistic humor.

"Take this uncouth heathen to the vault of misery, and be sure that his agonies are long and drawn out before death can release him."

"As you wish sire, your command shall be heeded immediately," answered the soldier on the right of Grignr as he stared into the barbarians seemingly unaffected face.

The advisor seated in the back of the noble slowly rose and advanced to the side of his master, motioning the wenches seated at his sides to remove themselves. He lowered his head and whispered to the noble.

"Eminence, the purnishment you have decreed will cause much misery to this scum, yet it will last only a short time, then release him to a land beyond the sufferings of the human body. Why not mellow him in one of the subterranean vaults for a few days, then send him to life labor in one of your buried mines. To one such

luxury and

echoing *[unnecessary hyphen]*

barbarian's

punishment

mines? *[missing question mark]*

he, a life spent in the confinement of the stygian pits
will be an infinitely more appropiate and lasting
torture."

The noble cupped his drooping double chin in the
folds of his briming palm, meditating for a moment upon
the rationality of the councilor's word's, then raised his
shaggy brown eyebrows and turned toward the advisor,
eyes aglow.

"...As always Agafnd, you speak with great wisdom.
Your words ring of great knowledge concerning the
nature of one such as he ," sayeth , the king. The noble
turned toward the prisoner with a noticable shimmer
reflecting in his frog-like eyes, and his lips contorting to
a greasy grin. "I have decided to void my previous decree.
The prisoner shall be removed to one of the palaces
underground vaults. There he shall stay until I have
decided that he has sufficiently simmered, whereupon he
is to be allowed to spend the remainder of his days at
labor in one of my mines."

Upon hearing this, Grignr realized that his fate would
be far less merciful than death to one such as he, who is
used to roaming the countryside at will. A life of
confinement would be more than his body and mind
could stand up to. This type of life would be
immeasurably worse than death.

"I shall never understand the ways if your twisted
civilization. I simply defend my honor and am condemned
to life confinement, by a pig who sits on his royal ass
wooing whores, and knows nothing of the affairs of the
land he imagines to rule!" Lectures Grignr ?

"Enough of this! Away with the slut before I loose my
control!"

appropriate

brimming [?]
words

unnecessary ellipsis   Agaphim

extra space before comma / unnecessary comma
noticeable

palace's

of

lectured   *question mark should be period*
lose

Seeing the peril of his position, Grignr searched for an opening. Crushing prudence to the sward, he plowed into the soldier at his left arm taking hold of his sword, and bounding to the dias supporting the prince before the startled guards could regain their composure. Agafnd leaped Grignr and his sire, but found a sword blade permeating the length of his ribs before he could loosed his weapon.

The councilor slumped to his knees as Grignr slid his crimsoned blade from Agfnd's rib cage. The fat prince stood undulating in insurmountable fear before the edge of the fiery maned comet, his flabs of jellied blubber pulsating to and fro in ripples of flowing terror.

"Where is your wisdom and power now, your magjesty?" Growled Grignr.

The prince went rigid as Grignr discerned him glazing over his shoulder. He swlived to note the cause of the noble's attention, raised his sword over his head, and prepared to leash a vicious downward cleft, but fell short as the haft of a steel rimed pike clashed against his unguarded skull. Then blackness and solitude. Silence enshrouding and ever peaceful reind supreme.

"Before me, sirrah! Before me as always! Ha, Ha Ha, Haaaa...", nobly cackled.

-3-

Consciousness returned to Grignr in stygmatic pools as his mind gradually cleared of the cobwebs cluttering its inner recesses, yet the stygian cloud of charcoal ebony remained. An incompatible shield of blackness, enhanced by the bleak abscense of sound.

sward (n.) – the grassy surface of land, turf

dais
Agaphim

permeate (v.) – to be diffused   loose
through; pervade; saturate

Agaphim's

majesty?" growled

swiveled

unleash
trimmed [?]

reigned

the noble

stygian

absence

Grignr's muddled brain reeled from the shock of the blow he had recieved to the base of his skull. The events leading to his predicament were slow to filter back to him. He dickered with the notion that he was dead and had descended or sunk, however it may be, to the shadowed land beyond the the aperature of the grave, but rejected this hypothesis when his memory sifted back within his grips. This was not the land of the dead, it was something infinitely more precarious than anything the grave could offer. Death promised an infinity of peace, not the finite misery of an inactive life of confined torture, forever concealed from the life bearing shafts of the beloved rising sun. The orb that had been before taken for granted, yet now cherished above all else. To be forever refused further glimpses of the snow capped summits of the land of his birth, never again to witness the thrill of plundering unexplored lands beyond the crest of a bleeding horizon, and perhaps worst of all the denial to ever again encompass the lustful excitement of caressing the naked curves of the body of a trim yound wench.

This was indeed one of the buried chasms of Hell concealed within the inner depths of the palace's despised interior. A fearful ebony chamber devised to drive to the brinks of insanity the minds of the unfortunately condemned, through the inapt solitude of a limbo of listless dreary silence.

-3½-

A tightly rung elliptical circle or torches cast their wavering shafts prancing morbidly over the smooth

received

extra "the"   aperture

young

[*Editor's note: inapt word choice*]

of

surface of a rectangular,ridged alter. Expertly chisled forms of grotesque gargoyles graced the oblique rim protruberating the length of the grim orifice of death, staring forever ahead into nothingness in complete ignorance of the bloody rites enacted in their prescence. Brown flaking stains decorated the golden surface of the ridge surrounding the alter, which banked to a small slit at the lower right hand corner of the altar. The slit stood above a crudely pounded pail which had several silver meshed chalices hanging at its sides. Dangling at the rim of golden mallet, the handle of which was engraved with images of twisted faces and groved at its far end with slots designed for a snug hand grip. The head of the mallet was slightly larger than a clenched fist and shaped into a smooth oval mass.

Encircling the marble altar was a congregation of leering shamen. Eerie chants of a bygone age, originating unknown eons before the memory of man, were being uttered from the buried recesses of the acolytes' deep lings. Orange paint was smeared in generous globules over the tops of thw Priests' wrinkled shaven scalps, while golden rings projected from the lobes of their pink ears. Ornate robes of lusciour purple satin enclosed their bulging torsos, attached around their waists with silvered silk lashes latched with ebony buckles in the shape of morose mis-shaped skulls. Dangling around their necks were oval fashoned medalions held by thin gold chains, featuring in their centers blood red rubys which resembled crimson fetish eyeballs. Cushoning their bare feet were plush red felt slippers with pointed golden spikes projecting from their tips.

Situated in front of the altar, and directly adjacent to the copper pail was a massive jade idol; a misshaped,

rectangular, ridged   altar   chiseled
protruding

presence
altar

"rimof" *should be* "rim was a"
grooved

shamans

lungs
the priests'

luscious

fashioned medallions
rubies
Cushioning

hideous bust of the shamens' pagan diety. The shimmering green idol was placed in a sitting posture on an ornately carved golden throne raised upon a round, dvory plated dias; it bulging arms and webbed hands resting on the padded arms of the seat. Its head was entwined in golden snake-like coils hanging over its oblong ears, which tappered off to thin hollow points. Its nose was a bulging triangular mass, sunken in at its sides with tow gaping nostrils. Dramatic beneath the nostrils was a twisted, shaggy lipped mouth, giving the impression of a slovering sadistic grimace.

At the foot of the heathen diety a slender, pale faced female, naked but for a golden, jeweled harness enshrouding her huge outcropping breasts, supporting long silver laces which extended to her thigh, stood before the pearl white field with noticable shivers traveling up and down the length of her exquisitely molded body. Her delicate lips trembled beneath soft narrow hands as she attemped to conceal herself from the piercing stare of the ambivalent idol.

Glaring directly down towards her was the stoney, cycloptic face of the bloated diety. Gaping from its single obling socket was scintillating, many fauceted scarlet emerald, a brilliant gem seeming to possess a life all of its own. A priceless gleaming stone, capable of domineering the wealth of conquering empires...the eye of Argon.

-4-

All knowledge of measuring time had escaped Grignr. When a person is deprived of the sun, moon, and stars, he looses all conception of time as he had previously

shamans'   deity

ivory   dais   its

tapered

two

slavering
deity

noticeable

attempted

stony
deity
oblong   was a scintillating   faceted
red beryl is sometimes marketed as "scarlet emerald";
true emeralds range from yellow-green to blue-green

loses

understood it. It seemed as if years had passed if time were being measured by terms of misery and mental anguish, yet he estimated that his stay had only been a few days in length. He has slept three times and had been fed five times since his awakening in the crypt. However, when the actions of the body are restricted its needs are also affected. The need for nourishmnet and slumber are directly proportional to the functions the body has performed, meaning that when free and active Grignr may become hungry every six hours and witness the desire for sleep every fifteen hours, whereas in his present condition he may encounter the need for food every ten hours, and the want for rest every twenty hours. All methods he had before depended upon were extinct in the dismal pit. Hence, he may have been imprisoned for ten minutes or ten years, he did not know, resulting in a disheartened emotion deep within his being.

The food, if you can honor the moldering lumps of fetid mush to that extent, was born to him by two guards who opened a portal at the top of his enclosure and shoved it to him in wooden bowls, retrieving the food and water bowels from his previous meal at the same time, after which they threw back the bolts on the iron latch and returned to their other duties. Since deprived of all other means of nourishment, Grignr was impelled to eat the tainted slop in order to ward off the paings of starvation, though as he stuffed it into his mouth with his filthy fingers and struggled to force it down his throat, he imagined it was that which had been spurned by the hounds stationed at various segments of the palace.

There was little in the baren vault that could occupy his body or mind. He had paced out the length and width

had

nourishment

borne

bowls

barren

of the enclosure time and time again and tested every granite slab which consisted the walls of the prison in hopes of finding a hidden passage to freedom, all of which was to no avail other than to keep him busy and distract his mind from wandering to thoughts of what he believed was his future. He had memorized the number of strides from one end to the other of the cell, and knew the exact number of slabs which made up the bleak dungeon. Numorous schemes were introduced and alternately discarded in turn as they succored to unravel to him no means of escape which stood the slightest chance of sucess.

Anguish continued to mount as his means of occupation were rapidly exhausted. Suddenly without no tive, he wasrouted from his contemplations as he detected a faint scratching sound at the end of the crypt opposite him. The sound seemed to be caused by something trying to scrape away at the grantite blocks the floor of the enclosure consisted of, the sandy scratching of something like an animal's claws.

Grignr gradually groped his way to the other end of the vault carefully feeling his way along with his hands ahead of him. When a few inches from the wall, a loud, penetrating squeal, and the scampering of small padded feet reverberated from the walls of the roughly hewn chamber.

Grignr threw his hands up to shield his face, and flung himself backwards upon his buttocks. A fuzzy form bounded to his hairy chest, burying its talons in his flesh while gnashing toward his throat with its grinding white teeth;its sour, fetid breath scortching the sqirming barbarians dilating nostrils. Grignr grappled with the

slab of which

Numerous

success

notice
was roused

granite

teeth; its   scorching   squirming
barbarian's

lashing flexor muscles of the repugnant body of a garganuan brownhided rat, striving to hold its razor teeth from his juicy jugular, as its beady grey organs of sight glazed into the flaring emeralds of its prey.

Taking hold of the rodent around its lean, growling stomach with both hands Grignr pried it from his crimson rent breast, removing small patches of flayed flesh from his chest in the motion between the squalid black claws of the starving beast. Holding the rodent at arms length, he cupped his righthand over its frothing face, contrcting his fingers into a vice-like fist over the quivering head. Retaining his grips on the rat, grignr flexed his outstretched arms while slowly twisting his right hand clockwise and his left hand counter clockwise motion. The rodent let out a tortured squall, drawing scarlet as it violently dug its foam flecked fangs into the barbarians sweating palm, causing his face to contort to an ugly grimace as he cursed beneath his braeth.

With a loud crack the rodents head parted from its squirming torso, sending out a sprinking shower of crimson gore, and trailing a slimy string of disjointed vertebrae, snapped trachea, esophagus, and jugular, disjointed hyoid bone, morose purpled stretched hide, and blood seared muscles.

Flinging the broken body to the floor, Grignr shook his blood streaked hands and wiped them against his thigh until dry, then wiped the blood that had showered his face and from his eyes. Again sitting himself upon the jagged floor, he prepared to once more revamp his glum meditations. He told himself that as long as he still breathed the gust of life through his lungs, hope was not lost; he told himself this, but found it hard to comprehend

gargantuan   brown-hided

arm's
right hand   contracting
vise
Grignr

squeal
barbarian's

breath
rodent's
sprinkling

purple

in his gloomy surroundings. Yet he was still alive, his bulging sinews at their peak of marvel, his struggling mind floating in a miral of impressed excellence of thought. Plot after plot sifted through his mind in energetic contemplations.

Then it hit him. Minutes may have passed in silent thought or days, he could not tell, but he stumbled at last upon a plan that he considered as holding a slight margin of plausibility.

He might die in the attempt, but he knew he would not submit without a final bloody struggle. It was not a foolproof plan, yet it built up a store of renewed vortexed energy in his overwroughtsoul, though he might perish in the execution of the escape, he would still be escaping the life of infinite torture in store forhim. Either way he would still cheat the gloating prince of the succored revenge his sadistic mind craved so dearly.

The guards would soon come to bear him off to the prince's buried mines of dread, giving him the sought after opportunity to execute his newly formulated plan. Groping his way along the rough floor Grignr finally found his tool in a pool of congealed gore; the carcass of the decapitated rodent; the tool that the very filth he had been sentenced too, spawned. When the time came for action he would have to be prepared, so he set himself to rending the sticky hulk in grim silence, searching by the touch of his fingertips for the lever to freedom.

-5-

"Up to the altar and be done with it wench;" ordered a fidgeting shaman as he gave the female a grim stare

morass *[?]*

vortex (n.) – a whirling mass of
air, water, fire...; a state of   overwrought soul
affairs likened to a whirlpool
for him
succor (n.) – help, relief, aid, assistance
succor (v.) – to help or relieve

to

wench,"

accompanied by the wrinkling of his lips to a mirthful grin of delight.

The girl burst into a slow steady whimper, stooping shakily to her knees and cringing woefully from the priest with both arms wound snake-like around the bulging jade jade shin rising before her scantily attired figure. Her face was redly inflamed from the salty flow of tears spouting from her glassy dilated eyeballs.

With short, heavy footfals the priest approached the female, his piercing stare never wavering from her quivering young countenance. Halting before the terrified girl he projected his arm outward and motioned her to arise with an upward movement of his hand. the girl's whimpering increased slightly and she sunk closer to the floor rather than arising. The flickering torches outlined her trim build with a weird ornate glow as it cast a ghostly shadow dancing in horrid waves of splendor over smoothly worn whiteness of the marble hewn altar.

The shaman's lips curled back farther, exposing a set of blackened, decaying molars which transformed his slovenly grin into a wide greasy arc of sadistic mirth and alternately interposed into the female a strong sensation of stomach curdling nausea. "Have it as you will female;" gloated the enhanced priest as he bent over at the waist, projecting his ape-like arms forward, and clasped the female's slender arms with his hairy round fists. With an inward surge of of his biceps he harshly jerked the trembling girl to her feet and smothered her salty wet cheeks with the moldy touch of his decrepid, dull red lips.

The vile stench of the Shaman's hot fetid breath over came the nauseated female with a deep soul searing sickness, causing her to wrench her head backwards and

doubled "jade"

footfalls

The

female,"

decrepit
shaman's   overcame

regurgitate a slimy, orange-white stream of swelling gore over the richly woven purple robe of the enthused acolyte.

The priest's lips trembled with a malicious rage as he removed his callous paws from the girl's arms and replaced them with tightly around her undulating neck, shaking her violently to and fro.

The girl gasped a tortured groan from her clamped lungs, her sea blue eyes bulging forth from damp sockets. Cocking her right foot backwards, she leashed it desperately outwards with the strength of a demon possessed, lodging her sandled foot squarely between the shaman's testicles.

The startled priest released his crushing grip, crimping his body over at the waist overlooking his recessed belly; wide open in a deep chasim. His face flushed to a rose red shade of crimson, eyelids fluttering wide with eyeballs protruding blindly outwards from their sockets to their outmost perimeters, while his lips quivered wildly about allowing an agonized wallow to gust forth as his breath billowed from burning lungs. His hands reached out clutching his urinary gland as his knees wobbled rapidly about for a few seconds then buckled, causing the ruptured shaman to collapse in an egg huddled mass to the granite pavement, rolling helplessly about in his agony.

The pathetic screeches of the shaman groveling in dejected misery upon the hand hewn granite laid pavement, worn smooth by countless hours of arduous sweat and toil, a welter of ichor oozing through his clenched hands, attracted the purturbed attention of his comrades from their foetid ulations. The actions of this this rebellious wench bespoke the creedence of an

replaced them with tightly *should be* placed them tightly

lashed

sandaled

chasm

perturbed
ululations
credence

unheard of sacrilige. Never before in a lost maze of untold eons had a chosen one dared to demonstrate such blasphemy in the face of the cult's idolic diety.

The girl cowered in unreasoning terror, helpless in the face of the emblazoned acolytes' rage; her orchid tusseled face smothered betwixt her bulging bosom as she shut her curled lashed tightly hoping to open them and find herself awakening from a morbid nightmare. yet the hand of destiny decreed her no such mercy, the antagonized pack of leering shaman converging tensely upon her prostrate form were entangled all too lividly in the grim web of reality.

Shuddering from the clamy touch of the shaman as they grappled with her supple form, hands wrenching at her slender arms and legs in all directions, her bare body being molested in the midst of a labyrnth of orange smudges, purpled satin, and mangled skulls, shadowed in an eerie crimson glow; her confused head reeled then clouded in a mist of enshrouding ebony as she lapsed beneath the protective sheet of unconsiousness to a land peach and resign.

-6-

"Take hold of this rope," said the first soldier, "and climb out from your pit, slut. Your presence is requested in another far deeper hell hole."

Grignr slipped his right hand to his thigh, concealing a small opaque object beneath the folds of the g-string wrapped about his waist. Brine wells swelled in Grignr's cold, jade squinting eyes, which grown accustomed to the gloom of the stygian pools of ebony engulfing him, were

sacrilege

idol-like *[?]*   deity

tousled

lashes
Yet

shamans

clammy   shamans

labyrinth
purple

unconsciousness

G-string

bedazzled and blinded by flickerering radiance cast forth by the second soldiers's resin torch.

Tightly gripped in the second soldier's right hand, opposite the intermittent torch, was a large double edged axe, a long leather wound oaken handled transfixing the center of the weapon's iron head. Adorning the torso's of both of the sentries were thin yet sturdy hauberks, the breatplates of which were woven of tightly hemmed twines of reinforced silver braiding. Cupping the soldiers' feet were thick leather sandals, wound about their shins to two inches below their knees. Wrapped about their waists were wide satin girdles, with slender bladed poniards dangling loosely from them, the hilts of which featured scarlet encrusted gems. Resting upon the manes of their heads, and reaching midway to their brows were smooth copper morions. Spiraling the lower portion of the helmet were short, up-curved silver spikes, while a golden hump spired from the top of each basinet. Beneath their chins, wound around their necks, and draping their clad shoulders dangled regal purple satin cloaks, which flowed midway to the soldiers feet.

hand over hand, feet braced against the dank walls of the enclosure, huge Grignr ascended from the moldering dephs of the forlorn abyss. His swelled limbs, stiff due to the boredom of a timeless inactivity, compounded by the musty atmosture and jagged granite protuberan against his body, craved for action. The opportunity now presenting itself served the purpose of oiling his rusty joints, and honing his dulled senses.

He braced himself, facing the second soldier. The sentry's stature was was wildly exaggerated in the glare of

flickering
soldier's

handle
torsos

breastplates

poinard (n.) – a small, slender dagger

morion (n.) – an open helmet of the 16th and 17th centuries

basinet (n.) – a globular or pointed helmet of the 14th century

soldiers'
Hand

depths   swollen

atmosphere   protuberance

doubled "was"

the flickering cresset cuppex in his right fist. His eyes were wide open in a slightly slanted owlish glaze, enhanced in their sinister intensity by the hawk-bill curve of his nose andpale yellow pique of his cheeks.

"Place your hands behind your back," said the second soldier as he raised his ax over his right shoulder blade and cast it a wavering glance. "We must bind your wrists to parry any attempts at escape. Be sure to make the knot a stout one, Broig, we wouldn't want our guest to take leave of our guidance."

Broig grasped Grignr's left wrist and reached for the barbarians's right wrist. Grignr wrenched his right arm free and swiveled to face Broig, reach- beneath his loin cloth with his right hand. The sentry grappled at his girdle for the sheathed dagger, but recoiled short of his intentions as Grignr's right arm swept to his gorge. The soldier went limp, his bobbing eyes rolling beneath fluttering eyelids, a deep welt across his spouting gullet. Without lingering to observe the result of his efforts, Grignr dropped to his knees. The second soldier's axe cleft over Grignr's head in a blze of silvered ferocity, severing several scarlet locks from his scalp. Coming to rest in his fellow's stomach, the iron head crashed through mail and flesh with splintering force, spilling a pool of crimsoned entrails over the granite paving.

Before the sentry could wrench his axe free from his comrade's carcass, he found Grignr's massive hands clasped about his throat, choking the life from his clamped lungs. With a zealous grunt, the Ecordian flexed his tightly corded biceps, forcing the grim faced soldier to one knee. The sentry plunged his right fist into Grignr's face, digging his grimy nails into the barbarians flesh.

cresset (n.) – a metal bowl filled   cupped
with oil for light

and pale

barbarian's
swiveled   reaching

blaze

barbarian's

Ejaculating a curse through rasping teeth, grignr surged the bulk of his weight foreard, bowling the beseiged soldier over upon his back. The sentry's arms collapsed to his thigh, shuddering convulsively; his bulging eyes staring blindly from a bloated ,cherry red face.

Rising to his feet, Grignr shook the bllod from his eyes, ruffling his surly red mane as a brush fire swaying to the nightime breeze. Stooping over the spr sprawled corpse of the first soldier, Grignr retrieved a small white object from a pool of congealing gore. Snorting a gusty billow of mirth, he once more concealed th e tiny object beneath his loin cloth; the tediously honed pelvis bone of the broken rodent. Returning his attention toward the second soldier, Grignr turned to the task of attiring his limbs. To move about freely through the dim recesses of the castle would require the grotesque garb of its soldiery.

Utilizing the silence and stealth aquired in the untamed climbs of his childhood, Grignr slink through twisting corridors, and winding stairways, lighting his way with the confisticated torch of his dispatched guardian. Knowing where his steps were leading to, Grignr meandered aimlessly in search of an exit from the chateau's dim confines. The wild blood coarsing through his veins yearned for the undefiled freedom of the livid wilderness lands.

Coming upon a fork in the passage he treaked, voices accompanied by clinking footfalls discerned to his sensitive ears from the left corridor. Wishing to avoid contact, Grignr veered to the right passageway. If aquested as to the purpose of his presence, his barbarous accent would reveal his identity, being that his attire was not that of the castle's mercenary troops.

Grignr
forward   besieged

thighs
bloated, cherry
blood

nighttime   *delete "spr"*

th e *should be* the

acquired
climes   slunk

confiscated

coursing

trekked

accosted

In grim silence Grignr treaded down the dingily lit corridor; a stalking panther creeping warily along on padded feet. After an interminable period of wandering through the dull corridors; no gaps to break the monotony of the cold gray walls, Grignr espied a small winding stairway. Descending the flight of arced granite slabs to their posterior, Grignr was confronted by a short haalway leading to a tall arched wooden doorway.

Halting before the teeming portal portal, Grignr restes his shaggy head sideways against the barrier. Detecting no sounds from within, he grasped the looped metel handle of the door; his arms surging with a tremendous effort of bulging muscles, yet the door would not budge. Retrieving his ax from where he had sheathed it beneath his girdle, he hefted it in his mighty hands with an apiesed grunt, and wedging one of its blackened edges into the crack between the portal and its iron rimed sill. Bracing his sandaled right foot against the rougjly hewn wall, teeth tightly clenched, Grignr appilevered the oaken haft, employing it as a lever whereby to pry open the barrier. The leather wound hilt bending to its utmost limits of endurance, the massive portal swung open with a grating of snapped latch and rusty iron hinges.

Glancing about the dust swirled room in the gloomily dancing glare of his flickering cresset, Grignr eyed evidences of the enclosure being nothing more than a forgotten storeroom. Miscellaneous articles required for the maintainance of a castle were piled in disorganized heaps at infrequent intervals toward the wall opposite the barbarian's piercing stare. Utilizing long, bounding strides, Grignr paced his way over to the mounds of supplies to discover if any articles of value were contained within their midst.

hallway

doubled "portal"   rested

metal

appeased *[?]*

roughly
applied

evidence

Detecting a faint clinking sound, Grignr sprawed to his left side with the speed of a striking cobra, landing harshly upon his back; torch and axe loudly clattering to the floor in a morass of sparks and flame. A elmwoven board leaped from collapsed flooring, clashing against the jagged flooring and spewing a shower of orange and yellow sparks over Grignr's startled face. Rising uneasily to his feet, the half stunned Ecordian glared down at the grusome arm of death he had unwittingly sprung. "Mrifk!"

If not for his keen auditory organs and lighting steeled reflexes, Grignr would have been groping through the shadowed hell-pits of the Grim Reaper. He had unknowingly stumbled upon an ancient, long forgotton booby trap; a mistake which would have stunted the perusal of longevity of one less agile. A mechanism, similar in type to that of a minature catapult was concealed beneath two collapsable sections of granite flooring. The arm of the device was four feet long, boasting razor like cleats at regular intervals along its face with which it was to skewer the luckless body of its would be victim. Grignr had stepped upon a concealed catch which relaesed a small metal latch beneath the two granite sections, causing them to fall inward, and thereby loose the spiked arm of death they precariously held in.

Partially out of curiosity and partially out of an inordinate fear of becoming a pincushion for a possible second trap, Grignr plunged his torch into the exposed gap in the floor. The floor of a second chamber stood out seven feet below the glare. Tossing his torch through the aperature, Grignr grasped the side of an adjoining tile, dropping down.

elm-woven *[?]*

gruesome

lightning steel

miniature

razor-like

would-be

aperture

Glancing about the room, Grignr discovered that he had decended into the palace's mausoleum. Rectangular stone crypts cluttered the floor at evenly placed intervals. The tops of the enclosures were plated with thick layers of virgin gold, while the sides were plated with white ivory; at one time sparkling, but now grown dingy through the passage of the rays of allencompassing mother time. Featured at the head of each sarcophagus in tarnished silver was an expugnisively carved likeness of its rotting inhabitant.

A dingy atmosphere pervaded the air of the chamber; which sealed in the enclosure for an unknown period had grown thick and stale. Intermingling with the curdled currents was the repugnant stench of slowly moldering flesh, creeping ever slowly but surely through minute cracks in the numerous vaults. Due to the embalming of the bodies, their flesh decayed at a much slower rate than is normal, yet the nauseous oder was none the less repellant.

Towering over Grignr's head was the trap he released. The mechanism of the miniaturized catapolt was cluttered with mildew and cobwebs. Notwithstanding these relics of antiquity, its efficiency remained unimpinged. To the right of the trap wound a short stairway through a recess in the ceiling; a concealed entrance leading to the mausoleum for which the catapult had obviously been erected as a silent, relentless guardian.

Climbing up the side of the device, Grignr set to the task of resetting its mechanism. In the e event that a search was organized, it would prove well to leave no evidence of his presence open to wandering eyes. Besides , it might even serve to dwindle the size of an opposing force.

all-encompassing

expugnisively – what?!

ever so slowly

odor   nonetheless

catapult

delete extraneous e

Besides,

Descending from his perch, Grignr was startled by a faintly muffled scream of horrified desperation. His hair prickled yawkishly in disorganized clumps along his scalp. As a cold danced along the length of his spinal cord. No moral/mortal barrier, human or otherwise, was capable of arousing the numbing sensation of fear inside of Grignr's smoldering soul. However, he was overwrought by the forces of the barbarians' instinctive fear of the supernatural. His mighty thews had always served to adequately conquer any tangible foe., but the intangible was something distant and terrible. Dim horrifying tales passed by word of mouth over glimmering camp fires and skins of wine had more than once served the purpose of chilling the marrowed core of his sturdy limbed bones.

Yet, the scream contained a strangely human quality, unlike that which Grignr imagined would come from the lungs of a demon or spirit, making Grignr take short nervous strides advancing to the sarcophagus from which the sound was issuing. Clenching his teeth in an attempt to steel his jangled nerves, Grignr slid the engraved slab from the vault with a sharp rasp of grinding stone. Another long drawn cry of terror infested anguish met the barbarian, scoring like the shrill piping of a demented banshee; piercing the inner fibres of his superstitious brain with primitive dread dread and awe.

Stooping over to espy the tomb's contents, the glittering Ecordians nostrills were singed by the scorching aroma of a moldering corpse, long shut up and fermenting; the same putrid scent which permeated the entire chamber, though multiplied to a much more concentrated dosage. The shriveled, leathery packet of

hawkishly *[?]*

foe,

marrow (n.) – a soft tissue inside bones

terror-infested

doubled "dread"

Ecordian's   nostrils

crumbling bones and dried flacking flesh offered no resistance, but remained in a fixed position of perpetual vigilance, watching over its dim abode from hollow gaping sockets.

The tortured crys were not coming from the tomb but from some hidden depth below! Pulling the reaking corpse from its resting place, Grignr tossed it to the floor in a broken, mangled heap. Upon one side of the crypt's bottom was attached a series of tiny hinges while running parallel along the opposite side of a convex railing like protruberance; laid so as to appear as a part of the interior surface of the sarcophagus.

Raising the slab upon its bronze hinges, long removed from the gaze of human eyes, Grignr percieved a scene which caused his blood to smolder not unlike bubbling, molten lava. Directly below him a whimpering female lay stretched upon a smooth surfaced marble altar. A pack of grasy faced shamen clustered around her in a tight circular formation. Crouched over the girl was a tall, potbellied priest; his face dominated by a disgusting, open mouthed grimace of sadistic glee. Suspended from the acolyte's clenched right hand was a carven oval faced mallet, which he waved menacingly over the girl's shadowed face; an incoherent gibberish flowing from his grinning, thick lipped mouth.

In the face of the amorphos, broad breated female, stretched out aluringly before his gaping eyes; the universal whim of nature filing a plea of despair inside of his white hot soul; Grignr acted in the only manner he could perceive. Giving vent to a hoarse, throat rending battle cry, Grignr plunged into the midst of the startled shamen; torch simmering in his left hand andax twirling in his right hand.

flaking

cries
reeking

protuberance

perceived

greasy   shamans

amorphous   breasted
alluringly
filling

shamans
and ax

A gaunt skull faced priest standing at the far side of the altar clutched desperately at his throat, coughing furiously in an attempt to catch his breath. Lurching helplessly to and fro, the acolyte pitched headlong against the gleaming base of a massive jade idol. Writhing agonizedly against the hideous image, foam flecking his chalk white lips, the priest struggled helplessly - - - the victim of an epileptic siezure.

Startled by the barbarians stunning appearance, the chronic fit of their fellow, and the fear that Grignr might be the avantgarde of a conquering force dedicated to the cause of destroying their degenerated cult, the saman momentarily lost their composure. Giving vent to heedless pandemonium, the priests fell easy prey to Grignr's sweeping arc of crimsoned death and maiming distruction.

The acolyte performing the sacrifice took a vicious blow to the stomach; hands clutching vitals and severed spinal cord as he sprawled over the altar. The disor anized priests lurched and staggered with split skulls, dismembered limbs, and spewing entrails before the enraged Ecordian's relentless onslaught. The howles of the maimed and dying reverberated against the walls of the tiny chamber; a chorus of hell frought despair; as the granite floor ran red with blood. The entire chamber was encompassed in the heat of raw savage butchery as Grignr luxuriated in the grips of a primitive, beastly blood lust.

Presently all went silenet save for the ebbing groans of the sinking shaman and Grignr's heaving breath accompanied by several gusty curses. The well had run dry. No more lambs remained for the slaughter.

The rampaging stead of death having taken of Grignr for the moment, left the barbarian free to the exploitation

skull-faced

chalk-white
seizure
barbarian's

*avant-garde (n.) – the advance group
in any field, especially in the visual,*   shamans
*literary, or musical arts, whose works
are characterized chiefly by
unorthodox and experimental methods.*   destruction

disorganized

howls

hell-fraught

silent
shamans

steed

of his other perusials. Towering over his head was the misshaped image of the cult's hideous diety - - - Argon. The fantastic size of the idol in consideration of its being of pure jade was enough to cause the senses of any man to stagger and reel, yet thus was not the case for the behemoth. he had paid only casual notice to this incredible fact, while riviting the whole of his attention upon the jewel protruding from the idol's sole socket; its masterfully cut faucets emitting blinding rays of hypnotising beauty. After all, a man cannot slink from a heavily guarded palace while burdened down by the intense bulk of a squatting statue, providing of course that the idol can even be hefted, which in fact was beyond the reaches of Grignr's coarsing stamina. On the other hand, the jewel, gigantic as it was, would not present a hinderence of any mean concern.

"Help me ... please ... I can make it well worth your while," pleaded a soft, anguish strewn voice wafting over Grignr's shoulders as he plucked the dull red emerald from its roots. Turning, Grignr faced the female that had lured him into this blood bath, but whom had become all but forgotten in the heat of the battle.

"You"; ejaculated the Ecordian in a pleased tone. "I though that I had seen the last of you at the tavern, but verilly I was mistaken." Grignr advanced into the grips of the female's entrancing stare, severing the golden chains that held her captive upon the altars highly polished face of ornamental limestone.

As Grignr lifted the girl from the altar, her arms wound dexterously about his neck; soft and smooth against his harsh exterior. "Art thou pleased that we have chanced to meet once again?" Grignr merely voiced an

perusals
deity

He

facets

coursing

hinderance

anguish strewn *should be* anguish-filled

"You,"

verily

altar's

sighed grunt, returning the damsels embrace while he smothered her trim, delicate lips between the coarsing protrusions of his reeking maw.

"Let us take leave of this retched chamber." Stated Grignr as he placed the female upon her feet. She swooned a moment, causing Grignr to giver her support then regained her stance. "Art thou able to find your way through the accursed passages of this castle? Mrifk! Every one of the corridors of this damned place are identical."

"Aye; I was at one time a slave of prince Agaphim. His clammy touch sent a sour swill through my belly, but my efforts reaped a harvest. I gained the pig's liking whereby he allowed me the freedom of the palace. It was through this means that I eventually managed escape of the palace.... It was a simple matter to seduce the sentry at the western gate. His trust found him with a dagger thrust his ribs," the wench stated whimsicoracally.

"What were you doing at the tavern whence I discovered you?" asked Grignr as he lifted the female through the opening into the mausoleum.

"I had sought to lay low from the palace's guards as they conducted their search for me. The tavern was seldom frequented by the palace guards and my identity was unknown to the common soldiers. It was through the disturbance that you caused that the palace guards were attracted to the tavern. I was dragged away shortly after you were escorted to the palace."

"What are you called by female?"

"Carthena, daughter of Minkardos, Duke of Barwego, whose lands border along the northwestern fringes of Gorzom. I was paid as homage to Agaphim upon his thirty-eighth year," husked the femme!

damsel's
coursing

wretched chamber," stated

give

thrust between his
whimsically *[?]*

Gorzam

"And I am called a barbarian!" Grunted Grignr in a disgusted tone!

"Aye! The ways of our civilization are in many ways warped and distorted, but what is your calling," she queried, bustily?

"Grignr of Ecordia."

"Ah, I have heard vaguely of Ecordia. It is the hill country to the far east of the Noregolean Empire. I have also heard Agaphim curse your land more than once when his troops were routed in the unaccustomed mountains and gorges." Sayeth she.

"Aye. My people are not tarnished by petty luxuries and baubles. They remain fierce and unconquerable in their native climes." After reaching the hidden panel at the head of the stairway, Grignr was at a loss in regard to its operation. His fiercest heaves were as pebbles against burnished armour! Carthena depressed a small symbol included within the elaborate design upon the panel whereopen it slowly slid into a cleft in the wall. "How did you come to be the victim of those crazed shamen?" Quested Grignr as he escorted Carthena through the piles of rummage on the left side of the trap.

"By Agaphim's orders I was thrust into a secluded cell to await his passing of sentence. By some means, the Priests of Argon acquired a set of keys to the cell. They slew the guard placed over me and abducted me to the chamber in which you chanced to come upon the scozsctic sacrifice. Their hell-spawned cult demands a sacrifice once every three moons upon its full journey through the heavens. They were startled by your unannounced appearance through the fear that you had been sent by Agaphim. The prince would surely have

Norgolian

whereupon
shamans

scozsctic – what?!

submitted them to the most ghastly of tortures if he had ever discovered their unfaithfulness to Sargon, his bastard diety. Many of the partakers of the ritual were high nobles and high trustees of the inner palace; Agaphim's pittiless wrath would have been unparalled."

"They have no more to fear of Agaphim now!" Bellowed Grignr in a deep mirthful tome; a gleeful smirk upon his face. "I have seen that they were delivered from his vengence."

Engrossed by Carthena's graceful stride and conversation Grignr failed to take note of the footfalls rapidly approaching behind him. As he swung aside the arched portal linking the chamber with the corridors beyond, a maddened, blood lusting screech reverberated from his ear drums. Seemingly utilizing the speed of thought, Grignr swiveled to face his unknown foe. With gaping eyes and widened jaws, Grignr raised his axe above his surly mein; but he was too late.

-7-

With wobbling knees and swimming head, the priest that had lapsed into an epileptic siezure rose unsteadily to his feet. While enacting his choking fit in writhing agony, the shaman was overlooked by Grignr. The barbarian had mistaken the siezure for the death throes of the acolyte, allowing the priest to avoid his stinging blade. The sight that met the priests inflamed eyes nearly served to sprawl him upon the floor once more. The sacrificial sat it grim, blood splattered silence all around him, broken only by the occasional yelps and howles of his maimed and butchered fellows. Above his head rose the hideous idol,

deity
pitiless
unparalleled

vengeance

mien

seizure

seizure

priest's

howls

its empty socket holding the shaman's ifurbished infuriated gaze.

His eyes turned to a stoney glaze with the realization of the pillage and blasphemy. Due to his high succeptibility following the siezure, the priest was transformed into a raving maniac bent soley upon reaking vengeance. With lips curled and quivering, a crust of foam dripping from them, the acolyte drew a long, wicked looking jewel hilted scimitar from his silver girdle and fled through the aperature in the ceiling uttering a faintly perceptible ceremonial jibberish.

-7½-

A sweeping scimitar swung towards Grignr's head in a shadowed blur of motion. With Axe raised over his head, Grignr prepared to parry the blow, while gaping wideeyed in open mouthed perplexity. Suddenly a sharp snap resounded behind the frothing shaman. The scimitar, halfway through its fatal sweep, dropped from a quivering nerveless hand, clattering harmlessly to the stoneage. Cutting his screech short with a bubbling, red mouthed gurgle, the lacerated acolyte staggered under the pressure of the released spring-board. After a moment of hopeless struggling, the shaman buckled, sprawling face down in a widening pool of bllod and entrails, his regal purple robe blending enhancingly with the swirling streams of crimson.

"Mrifk! I thought I had killed the last of those dogs;" muttered Grignr in a half apathetic state.

"Nay Grignr. You doubtless grew careless while giving vent to your lusts. But let us not tarry any long lest

delete "ifurbished"

susceptibility   seizure
solely   wreaking

aperture
gibberish

axe

wide-eyed   open-mouthed

stoneage – what?!
red-mouthed

blood
enchantingly *[?]*

dogs,"

longer

we over tax the fates. The paths leading to freedom will soon be barred. The wretch's crys must certainly have attracted unwanted attention," the wench mused.

"By what direction shall we pursue our flight?"

"Up that stair and down the corridor a short distance is the concealed enterance to a tunnel seldom used by others than the prince, and known to few others save the palace's royalty. It is used mainly by the prince when he wishes to take leave of the palace in secret. It is not always in the Prince's best interests to leave his chateau in public view. Even while under heavy guard he is often assaulted by hurtling stones and rotting fruits. The commoners have little love for him." lectured the nerelady!

"It is amazing that they would ever have left a pig like him become their ruler. I should imagine that his people would rise up and crucify him like the dog he is."

"Alas, Grignr, it is not as simple as all that. His soldiers are well paid by him. So long as he keeps their wages up they will carry out his damned wished. The crude impliments of the commonfolk would never stand up under an onslaught of forged blades and protective armor; they would be going to their own slaughter," stated Carthena to a confused, but angered Grignr as they topped the stairway.

"Yet how can they bear to live under such oppression? I would sooner die beneath the sword than live under such a dog's command." added Grignr as the pair stalked down the hall in the direction opposite that in which Grignr had come.

"But all men are not of the same mold that you are born of, they choose to live as they are so as to save their filthy necks from the chopping block." Returned Carthena

overtax
cries

entrance

prince's

him,"   *nerelady – what?!*
let

implements   common folk

command,"

block," returned

in a disgusted tone as she cast an appiesed glance towards
the stalwart figure at her side whose left arm was wound
dextrously about her slim waist; his slowly waning torch
casting their images in intermingling wisps as it dangled
from his left hand.

Presently Carthena came upon the panel, concealed
amonst the other granite slabs and discernable only by the
burned out cresset above it. "As I push the cresset aside
push the panel inwards." Catrhena motioned to the panel
she was refering to and twisted the cresset in a
counterclockwise motion. Grignr braced his right
shoulder against the walling, concentrating the force of
his bulk against it. The slab gradually swung inward with
a slight grating sound. Carthena stooped beneath Grignr's
corded arms and crawled upon all fours into the passage
beyond. Grignr followed after easing the slab back into
place.

Winding before the pair was a dark musty tunnel,
exhibiting tangled spider webs from it ceiling to wall and
an oozing, sickly slime running lazily upon its floor.
Hanging from the chipped wall upon GrignR's right side
was a half mouldered corpse, its grey flacking arms held
in place by rusted iron manacles. Carthena flinched back
into Grignr's arms at sight of the leering set in an ugly
distorted grimmace; staring horribly at her from hollow
gaping sockets.

"This alcove must also be used by Agaphim as a
torture chamber. I wonder how many of his enemies have
disappeared into these haunts never to be heard from
again," pondered the hulking brute.

"Let us flee before we are also caught within
Agaphim's ghastly clutches. The exit from this tunnel

appiesed – what?!

dextrously

amongst

referring

wall

its

Grignr's
flaking

at the sight
grimace

cannot be very far from here!" Said Carthena with a slight sob to her voice, as she sagged in Grignr's encompasing embrace.

"Aye; It will be best to be finished with this corridor as soon as it is possible. But why do you flinch from the sight of death so? Mrift! You have seen much death this day without exhibiting such emotions." Exclaimed Grignr as he led her trembling form along the dingy confines.

"---The man hanging from the wall was Doyanta. He had committed the folly of showing affections for me in front of Agaphim --- he never meant any harm by his actions!" At this Carthena broke into a slow steady whimpering, chokking her voice with gasping sobs. "There was never anything between us yet Agaphim did this to him! The beast! May the demons of Hell's deepest haunts claw away at his wretched flesh for this merciless act!" she prayed.

"I detect that you felt more for this fellow than you wish to let on ... but enough of this, We can talk of such matters after we are once more free to do so." With this Grignr lifted the grieved female to her feet and strode onward down the corridor, supporting the bulk of her weight with his surging left arm.

Presently a dim light was perceptibly filtering into the tunnel, casting a dim reddish hue upon the moldy wall of the passage's grim confines. Carthena had ceased her whimpering and partially regained her composure. "The tunnel's end must be nearing. Rays of sunlight are beginning to seep into ..."

Grignr clameed his right hand over Carthena's mouth and with a slight struggle pulled her over to the shadows at the right hand wall of the path, while at the same time

said
encompassing

"Aye, it

Mrifk!
emotions," exclaimed

choking

thrusting this torch beneath an overhanging stone to smother its flickering rays. "Be silent; I can hear footfalls approaching through the tunnel;" growled Grignr in a hushed tone.

"All that you hear are the horses corraled at the far end of the tunnel. That is a further sign that we are nearing our goal." She stated!

"All that you hear is less than I hear! I heard footsteps coming towards us. Silence yourself that we may find out whom we are being brought into contact with. I doubt that any would have thought as yet of searching this passage for us. The advantage of surprize will be upon our side." Grignr warned.

Carthena cast her eyes downward and ceased any further pursuit towards conversation, an irritating habit in which she had gained an amazing proficiency. Two figures came into the pairs view, from around a turn in the tunnel. They were clothed in rich luxuriant silks and rambling o on in conversation while ignorant of their crouching foes waiting in an ambush ahead.

"...That barbarian dog is cringing beneath the weight of the lash at this moment sire. He shall cause no more disturbance."

"Aye, and so it is with any who dare to cross the path of Sargon's chosen one." said the 2nd man.

"But the peasants are showing signs of growing unrest. They complain that they cannot feet their families while burdened with your taxes."

"I shall teach those sluts the meaning of humility! Order an immediate increase upon their taxes. They dare to question my sovereign authority, Ha-a, they shall soon learn what true oppression can be. I will ... "

tunnel,"

corralled

goal," she stated.

surprise will be on our side," Grignr warned.

pair's

delete extraneous o

moment, sire.

one,"   second

feed

A shodowed bulk leapt from behind a jutting promontory as it brought down a double edged axe with the spped of a striking thought. One of the nobles sagged lifeless to the ground, skull split to the teeth.

Grignr gasped as he observed the bisected face set in its leering death agonies. It was Agafnd! The dead mans comrade having recovered from his shock drew a jewel encrusted dagger from beneath the folds of his robe and lunged toward the barbarians back. Grignr spun at the sound from behind and smashed down his crimsoned axe once more. His antagonist lunged howling to a stream of stagnent green water, grasping a spouting stump that had once been a wrist. Grignr raised his axe over his head and prepaired to finish the incomplete job, but was detered half way through his lunge by a frenzied screech from behind.

Carthena leapt to the head of the writhing figure, plunging a smoldering torch into the agonized face. The howls increased in their horrid intensity, stifled by the sizzling of roasting flesh, then died down until the man was reduced to a blubbering mass of squirming, insensate flesh.

Grignr advance to Carthena's side wincing slightly from the putrid aroma of charred flesh that rose in a puff of thick white smog throughout the chamber. Carthena reeled slightly, staring dasedly downward at her gruesome handywork. "I had to do it ... it was Agaphim ... I had to, " she exclaimed!

"Sargon should be more carful of his right hand men." Added Grignr, a smug grin upon his lips. "But to hell with Sargon for now, the stench is becoming bothersome to me." With that Grignr grasped Carthena around the waist leading her around the bend in the cave and into the open.

shadowed
double-edged
speed

Agaphim   man's
jewel-encrusted

barbarian's

stagnant

deterred

advanced

dazedly
handiwork
to,"
careful

A ball of feral red was rising through the mists of the eastern horizon, disipating the slinking shadows of the night. A coral stood before the pair, enclosing two grazing mares. Grignr reached into a weighted down leather pouch dangling at his side and drew forth the scintillant red emerald he had obtained from the bloated idol. Raising it toward the sun he said, "We shall do well with bauble, eh!"

Carthena gaped at the gem gasping in a terrified manner "The eye of Argon, Oh! Kalla!" At this the gem gave off a blinding glow, then dribbled through Grignr's fingers in a slimy red ooze. Grignr stepped back, pushing Carthena behind him. The droplets of slime slowly converged into a pulsating jelly-like mass. A single opening transfixed the blob, forminf into a leechlike maw.

Then the hideous transgressor of nature flowed towards Grignr, a trail of greenish slime lingering behind it. The single gap puckered repeatedly emitting a ghastly sucking sound.

Grignr spread his legs into a battle stance, steeling his quivering thews for a battle royal with a thing he knew not how to fight. Carthena wound her arms about her protectors neck, mumbling, "Kill it! Kill!" While her entire body trembled.

The thing was almost upon Grignr when he buried his axe into the gristly maw. It passed through the blob and clanged upon the ground. Grignr drew his axe back with a film of yellow-green slime clinging to the blade. The thing was seemingly unaffected. Then it started to slooze up his leg. The hairs upon his nape stoode on end from the slimey feel of the things buly, bulk. The Nautous

feral (adj.) – of or characteristic of
dissipating   *wild animals; ferocious; brutal*
corral

with this bauble

Eye

forming

protector's

ooze
stood
slimy   thing's burly bulk   nauseating

sucking sound became louder, and Grignr felt the blood being drawn from his body. With each hiss of hideous pucker the thing increased in size.

Grignr shook his foot about madly in an attempt to dislodge the blob, but it clung like a leech, still feeding upon his rapidly draining life fluid. He grasped with his hands trying to rip it off, but only found his hands entangled in a sickly gluelike substance. The slimey thing continued its puckering ; now having grown the size of Grignr's leg from its vampiric feast.

Grignr began to reel and stagger under the blob, his chalk white face and faltering muscles attesting to the gigantic loss of blood. Carthena slipped from Grignr in a death-like faint, a morrow chilling scream upon her red rubish lips. In final desperation Grignr grasped the smoldering torch upon the ground and plunged it into the reeking maw of the travestry. A shudder passed through the thing. Grignr felt the blackness closing upon his eyes, but held on with the last ebb of his rapidly waning vitality. He could feel its grip lessoning as a hideous gurgling sound erupted from the writhing maw. The jelly like mass began to bubble like a vat of boiling tar as quivers passed up and down its entire form.

- The lost ending -

With a sloshing plop the thing fell to the ground, evaporating in a thick scarlet cloud until it reatained its original size. It remained thus for a moment as the puckered maw took the shape of a protruding red eyeball, the pupil of which seemed to unravel before it the tale of creation. How a shapeless mass slithered from the

slimy
puckering;   grown to the

marrow-chilling
ruby *[assuming the author meant rubyish]*

travesty

lessening

reattained

quagmires of the stygmatic pool of time, only to degenerate into a leprosy of avaricious lust. In that fleeting moment the grim mystery of life was revealed before Grignr's ensnared gaze.

The eyeballs glare turned to a sudden plea of mercy, a plea for the whole of humanity. Then the blob began to quiver with violent convulsions; the eyeball shattered into a thousand tiny fragments and evaporated in a curling wisp of scarlet mist. The very ground below the thing began to vibrate and swallow it up with a belch.

The thing was gone forever. All that remained was a dark red blotch upon the face of the earth, blotching things up. Shaking his head, his shaggy mane to clear the jumbled fragments of his mind, Grignr tossed the limp female over his shoulder. Mounting one of the disgruntled mares, and leading the other; the weary, scarred barbarian trooted slowly off into the horizon to become a tiny pinpoint in a filtered filed of swirling blue mists, leaving the Nobles, soldiers and peasants to replace the missing monarch. Long leave the king !!!!

eyeball's   plea for mercy

vibrate, and swallowed

trotted
field
nobles
live

The Return of the Eye of Argon
Hildy Silverman

After a time of happy briefness spent with Carthena, Grignr tired of his orchid-tresed wench and departed for new adventure in the far-off towne of Nogra. Her sorrow at the departure of the scarletmaned giant was eased by the muscular masculine infant she'd borne following Grignr's frequent ministrations.

"Mrifk!" Exclaimed the barbarous male as he past through the golden gates of Nogra. "Surely such a place has need of a protector of my stature"? For Grignr's purse had withered during his travels, and he was in sore need of coin for food and wenches.

He steered his stead through the winding streets of the lush township, noting the well-appointed abodes and shoppes windows filled with jewels, sweets, silken garb, playthings, and other elements which bespoke much wealth. Finanly he arrive at the largest chateau whichwas owned by the famed mighty lord of Nogra.

Dismounting his mount, Grignr tied the wholesome beast to a post and went to knock upon the lord's door. But before his clenched digits could rap upon the mahogany wood, the door sprang open! A stegosaurian voice from within beckoned, "Welcome, o mighty babarian. We have been expecting you."

Grignr felt a shiver of caution coarse down his spine. Nevertheless, he stepped across the threshold and into the stragely darkened house. He squinted perturbedly into the stygian debts. "Mrifk! I cannot see my hand before my visage," grumbled the annoyed barbarian!

"Forgive me." The silvered tongued speaker evaporated out of the blackness before Grignr holding a small torch in his hand. He bowed his bald oval. "I am Renflad, servant to Lord Drala. He wishes me to escort you to his room of greeting." The scrawny male pointed to the length of hall behind him. "If you would please followme?"

Despite his misreadings, Grignr followed the torch-baring server down the hallway. His keen ears perked at the sounds coming from behind closed doors along the way. The noises of merry coupling reached him from one, while another bore the sounds of painfilled moans and groans to his concerned earholes. Grignr narrowed his emerald orbs in concentration and placed one huge paw on the hilt of his sword.

The bare-pate waved Grignr into the lords vaulted marbeledgreatroom. The cavernous space was filled with couches of velvets and fine woods, rocks-slab tables, and paintings of love acts so bold and lewd that even Grignr averted his orbs from observing them too closely. Torches set about the space lit it up.

At the far end of the parlour sat a towering male clad in silver-grey pelts upon a thronelike chair of marbles and cushions. His long greasey hair hung to his pointed nipples and his globes of vision faintly paled red.

A female with grainy-yellow waves of hair sat at his feet. Only her pleasure cove was covered by a golden-mesh loincloth; otherwise her snowy complexion was visible to all with the fortitude to gaze upon it. Her face was set in a gaze of weary acceptance.

"Greetings, Grignr of Ecordia, or should I say Gorzom." Queried the noble? "Welcome to my domicile."

Grignr grunted and approached the throned man. "Tell me how you know so much of me when I merely happened upon this realm!"

The nobleman smiles revealed pointy sharp teeth that were shiny in the torch-light. "I am Lord Drala of Nogra," he simpered. "My reach extends far beyond my domain. My spies have observed your traveles and correctly insinuated that you would bedrawn here by our many delights." He caressed the long twines of his woman's hair with one pointy nailed hand.

Grignr did not care for the thought that he had been observed or for this disturbing nobles imprications. "What is it you want from me?" he demanded.

"Why, only to give you the honours you have earned" Purred the lord cattily. "You are the worthy who destroyed the cursed Eye of Argon, are you not?"

Grignr crossed his thick arms across his bulging pectorals. "I did. I also slew the wicked cult of Argon and the gelatinous prince of Gorzom. What of it!"

Lord Darla claped his palms together. "We are greatfull, good barbarian! Those Argonian sluts stole that mystical scarlet emerald from our protection, you see, and thrust it betwixt their cursed idol's socket. They had no right to its power only one such as I can properly weld it," instructed the lord.

"The gem is no more." Grignr tossed his scarlet plumes behind his massive shoulders. "It melted away before me."

"So it did." The Lord rose and stepped down from his throne and stood in front of it and Grignr. "But what you do not understand is what hapened to it next. You see, the essence of the Eye flowed through the sands and made its way back to its rightfull master. Me!"

Drala pulled apart the furs obscuring his chest and revealed a thick golden chain hung with a many-fauceted stone that glowed red as fire. It was the Eye of Argon!

Grignr gasped and drew his sword. "No not that again! How many times must I destroy it?" wondered the concerned giant.

Guards suddenly flowed into the throneroom from all sides. Garbed in leatherarmour and waving swords they advanced on the upset barbarian in their midst. But then Lord Dralaraised his hand and cried. "Do not attack my guest!" Commanded the tall one. "He simply misunderstands. Grignr, the Eye is no threat to you or anyone else now that it has come home."

"Lies?" Growled the enthused hero. "It transformed into a large sucking thing and tried to drain my lifefluids!"

"Perhaps, but it is tamed now." Dralastrocked the gemstone like a pet rock. "The Eye chose you, do you not see? It thought you worthy to become one of my kind and so attempted to foist upon you the dark gift."

"What is this nonsense you spew" Grignr looked around the room and noticed that the guards were smiling with teeth like scimitars.

Drala was suddenly very close to Grignr looking down at him from a head or so above with his bright red orbs. "Your might makes you a perfect candidate for our brotherhood of blood." He explained. "Join us willingly and I will make you my second in command. You will know delights and riches beyond reckoning, forever!"

Grignr's mind swilveled with thoughts. On the one hand, a life of leisure and cash that never ended was tempting. But on the other, he knew nothing was ever easy or free. Plus the boredom of lying about for eternity did not appeal to his adventuresome nature.

"I do not want these," Grignr explained with a shrug. "What is life if not put at risk from time to time? What is wealth that has not been wrested by force of will? What is having many wenches if have not been seduced with effort?"

"I did not mention wenches," frowned the noble.

Grignr ignored him. "I only ask to be free to roam this world and indulge in its pleasures earned at the point of my sword." He spread his bulky corded limbs wide. "You are all alike, you nobells. Soft," Grignr ejaculated furiously!

Lord Drala sighed. "Very well. You disappoint me, wild one. I had hoped to add your strength to my peoples' but if not, then you must sadly be destroyed for rejecting the Eye of Argon's blessing. Guards?" He undulated at his men and they surged forward.

Grignr swung his blade. It clanged against the tanned skin amour of the first guard with enough force to knock him to the ground. Swinging his sword up and behind him, the barbarian's mighty thews drove the blade deep into the gut of a guardsman at his back. But although he managed to slash and pierce several of the guards with what should have been death blows, the members of the excited throng kept springing back up to surround him again and again.

"What witchery is this?" Grignr exploded with frustration.

"Behold, the power you so foolishly snubbed!" Lord Drala sneered. He strolled back toward his throne but turned around to watch the battle from a safe distance. "My men are not so easily thwarted as that fool Agaphim's! Now you see how mere steel has no lasting affect on immortals"?

Grignr began to worry that the towering princeling told the truth. He found himself backed up against one marble wall beneath the painting of a trio of females drinking the blood of a nude man. Oh, Cartheena, Grignr's racing mind remembered. If only I had remained with you and our sinewy babe!

Suddenly, a woman's voice pierced through the cacophonous battle. "Their heads, mighty barbarian," proclaimed the woman seated by Drala's throne. She rose to her bear feet. "Remove them and you can yet prevail!"

"Silence faithless concubine!" Drala slapped the brazen yellow-haired across her snowy cheek knocking her to the floor.

Firey tresses flinging forward furiously, Grignr released a battle cry and began obeying the fallen wenche's advice. He sliced off the screeching head of one foe as an experiment. Sure enough, the startled oval rolled to the floor and lay still while his body ceased forward motion and collapsed. It worked!

Grignr set his jaw and began hacking and slicing every neck that had the misfortune to approach his blade. Although the guards managed to impart the raging giant with some scratches and jabs, they soon fell before his berserk assault. At last, the floor ran scarlet with blood and strewn with heads atop ragged neck-stems that once attached to living beings.

Panting with effort, Grignr fixed his glaring vision on Lord Drala. "By the surly beard of Mrifk, your head shall join there's, wicked creature" He conjectured.

The disturbed lord bared his mouth of knife-like teeth and hissed. "Come meet your doom, then! I am the master of my kind and you'll find my head much harder to separate from my anatomy!"

Grignr roared like a starving giraffe and ran at Lord Drala. But just as he approached, the terrifying nobal sprang into the air and transformed into a gigantic silver-grey wolf. Grignr was very surprised!

The wolf clamped its jaws around the Ecordian's corded fourarmand forced him to drop his blade. Screaming from pain, Grignr pounded the top of the wolf's skull with his meaty fist, to no avail. The wolf boar him to the floor where they wrestled, glowing scarlet orbs locked with wide green ones.

Grignr felt himself weakening as his veins were drained of vital fluids by the wolf's fangs. He began to pray to his burly god Mrifk, the buxom goddess Mrafk, and their myriad siblings including Mrefk, Mrofk, Mrufk, and Mryfk for succor. But just as his sight began misting over, the wolf released an agonizing howl.

Grignr blinked and beheld the lord's captive wench astride the wolf's back. Her delicate digits were wrapped around the hilt of a knife that gleamed silver in the reflected torchlight. She plunged it into the side of the wolf's neck again and again causing rich dark red blackness to squirt from the punctures. Her busts bounced beguilingly as she attacked. "Die, evil creature, die!" Screamed the damsel.

Grignr groped until his desperate fingertips found his fallen weapon. He grabbed the hilt and swung his blade sideways into the bemused head of the wolf. It's head half-off, the beast reared backward throwing the erstwhile femme aside. The wolf shuddered and vanished leaving the bloddypelt-coated Lord Drala in its place.

"Mercy?" begged the gushing unworthy of Grignr as he clasped his hands to his almost severaled neck.

Grignr thew his head back and laughed. "Bah! Not so aloof now, my lord, eh? I shall gift you the only mercy you deserve… a quick death!" With that he chopped down and cut the lord's perturbed skull entirely off. It bounced once and then rolled to a stop by Grignr's big toe.

"Well done mighty one!" Cried the wench. She stood up and swept her wheat-coloured twines away from her pasty features. "I have waited so long for one such as you with the fortitude to end this bilious yokel's reign."

"I thank you for your sage consultations." Grignr took the maid by her shoulders and pulled her unresisting figure close. She ran her hands across his veiny pectorals and down over his firm, flat abdominus. "But how came you to be in the thrall of this wicked fool?"

Her ruby lips parted as she explained. "I am the Lady Lucina of the royal house of Vanarker. I was sent here to seduce the bloodthirsty lord you have most hastily dispatched in hopes that I would get the chance to slay him and free my people of the tyranny of Nogra. The people of this town have grown rich and fat off the blood and wealth of their neighbors under Drala's leadership. But I did not get an opportunity to strike until you happened along. O, most fortunate day!"

"Indeed." Grignr smothered her smiling maw with his slavering lips. She twinned her dainty limbs about him and moaned her pleasure.

After a time, Grignr drew back. He wondered, "What of the others in this palace? I heard sounds behind the doors and not all were joyful."

"This is where the bloated tics bring victims to drain." Shuddered the girl. "Some think they are here to be made love to but all quickly learn they are naught but food."

"Monstors." Grignr raised his sword and turned to leave. "I shall end every last one of them"?

"Go forth, mighty one," enthused Lucina. "I shall follow you. But first." She reached down and picked up the fauceted crimson emerald, now sticky with Drala's blood.

Grignr flinched. "Leave that," he pronounced.

"Do not fear. My people know how to manage this bloodsucking fiend." She pressed her silver knife against the cursed gem and began muttering a stream of gibberish. Finally she said, "There. It is bound and cannot shift its form any longer. I will take it to my homeland where it will be cast into the fires of Ice Giants!"

Grignr shrugged and hustled away to kick in the doors of the chateau and remove the heads of the evil ones within. Lucina trailed in his wake and rejoiced, for the curse of the Eye of Argon was at last broken and would plague humanity no more!

The Rat's Tail
Keith R.A. DeCandido

The rat waited.

The hirsute creature paced the stuygian depths of the dungeon beneath the castle. For its entire short life it had paced the stoney floor of the dark and dank dungeon, eating whatever scraps might find their way to his ravenous gullet.

Every once in a while there was a prisoner, and the rat would rejoice fondily, for ineviably there would be food for the prisoner. The food was always incredibly terrrible and the prisoner wouldn't eat it. Sometimes the prisoner would not eat on moral grounds, objecting to the very concept of being a prisoner. Sometimes the prisoner just didn't like the food.

The rat didn't care one wsay or the other, it5 just enjoyed eating the leftovers. It would have long since straved, otherwise.

Of course, thebest part, the absolute best, was when the prisoners died. Then the rat could eat for weeks!

As a result of gorging itself on the corpses of prisoners and the scraps of foodstuffs left carelessly behind, the rat had grtown to be absolutely huge. Its talons had grown sharp as knives and its teeth the likewise same.

But then a long time past between prisones. The rat started to grow forlorn and upset.

And so the rat waited.

And waited some more.

It started to get hungry. The last prisoner had been very fat, so the rat had stored a great deal of food in its gullet from the obese jailbird sent down by the king.

Sometimes, when it was starving so much, it would recall a previous life that it lived. A previous life that was only the dimmest of memories buried deep in the rat's cerebellum. A time that was so far in the past it seemed like it taked place in another space-time continuum entirely.

A time when it was ahuman man named Forgnd, instead of an animal rat with no name to call his own.

Long ago, so long ago that Forgnd had no idea how many years it was, trapped as he had been in his rodentian form in the obsidian depths of the castle dungeon, the rat was a man. Advisor to the king, he was, and the king always took Forgnd's sage advise on matters of import to the throen.

But then the king died when he choked on a hicken bone, and his corpulent son ascended to the kindship in his stead. From that moment on, everything went very poorly for everyone in the kingdom, for the new king was a fool and an imbecile. Instead of listening to Forgnd, who had been his father's most trusted advistor, he instead started paying more attention to the priests and also to a weaselly psychophant named Agafnd.

One day, Forgnd exploded in rage, telling Agafnd that the king was an idiot for not taking his advice. To Forgn'ds horror and shame, Agafnd immediately told the king of his outburst. The king did not take that very well, and ordered the royal mage to turn Forgnd into a rat. Agafnd took over as the king's advisor, and Forgnd was banished to the nether reachers of the castle, never to see the light of day or walk on his own two feet again.

For years, the rat had survived on scraps and corpses. But time had passed interminably in the dungeon and it despaired of ever getting a proper meal again.

And so the rat wiated.

Then the barbarian arrived.

The rat rejoiced, for at last there would be food!

Sure enough, the guards brought the delicious foodstuffs that they always delivered to the prisons. The rat looked forward to eating it—but then the barbarian ate it! All of it!

Disappoitned, the rat started t opace the dungeon, wondering who this creqature was. Obviously he was someone who had offended the king, but why then did he eat the food? What land could this man have come from that he thought the vile foodstuffs were worthyof being consumed?

Had the rat still been human, had it still been Forgnd, he would have found the food to be revolting. But he was a rat now, and rats loved bad food.

Usually the prisoners avoided the food. If not the first, time, then definitely the second time and beyond.

But this stupid barbarian kept eating!

The rat was starving now, and desperate for food.

Maybe the barbarian would die soon?

Or maybe he would be taken away.

The rat could'nt take it anymore.

It leaped onto th4 barbarian and knocked him to the floor.

The former Forgnd intended to show the barbarian what for.

The barbarian was feeling his way along the walls in a futile quest to find an egress. The rat laughed at the barbarians' foolish endeavor, doomed as it was to abject failure. There was no way out of the prison. Forgnd himself had been one of the designers of the dungeon back when the previous king was still alive, and he knew it was completely impossible to escape from for anyone.

Leaping with a squeal, the rat attacked the Barbarian, who threw up his hands and fell backwards on to his gluteus maximum. Digging its talons into the barbarian's chest, the rat made to bite the man's neck, eagerly looking forward to the salty taste of the blood flowing through his carotid artery.

However, to the rat's overweening surprise, it ws unable to close the deal, as it were, as the barbarian's French-loaf-sized hands clasped around the rat's torso and retarded its forward motion towards the barbarian's neck area.

The rat squirmed ,attempting t obreak free of the barbarian's visiouc hold on its person. Sadly, even as the rat struggle dmightily to break the barbarbians grip, the big man's right hand clamped down on the rat's face.

The erstwhile Forgnd was outraged. How dare this pitiful barbarian manhandle him this way? Or may be it should have been rat-handled him? Irregardless, the rat thrashed and jumped and tried to escape the barbarians' fateful grip.

And then the barbarian's right hand started to move in a clockwise motion , even as his left hand moved counterclockwise.

The rat laughed heartily in its mind. Truly, this barbarian was a great fool indeed! Moving his arms that way would just cause his arms to hit each other, and he'd neve rbe able to achieve the momentum necessary to crack the rat's neck!

What a complete fool!

Those were the last thoughts that past through the rat's brainpan, for a microsecond later, despite the poor leverage of his twist, the barbarian managed to separate the rat's head from the rest of its body, its disjointed vertebrae, snapped trachea, esophagus, and jugular, disjointed hyoid bone, morose purpled stretched hide, and blood seared muscles flying across the stony dungeon floor.

The rat waited no more. The last vestige of the previous king was now a bloody, gory mess on the stone floor.

Forgnd the rat died, but at least he did not die in vain, for his murderer was unbenownwst tohim, Grignr, the mighty barbarian from Ecordia. Before long, Grignr would do the impossible and escape the inescapable dungeon, and—using one of the rat's bones as a weapon—he would take advantaege of his fgreedome to bring about the destruction of the hated king.

So while the rat died an ignominious death, it also died in a cause that would lead to the destruction of its most hated enemy.

Grignr and the Dragnr
Peter Prellwitz

Chapter 1

The cold was very cold. Grignr herdalded the cold night with his grunting sinnews barking at the very cold. With mighty clopping, Grignrs horse steed braved the coldness. "Forsoth, brave journer mate! Thou art worthy of companonship should ere we live! But HO! what is that Isee in the cold disntats?"

Behold! It were an inne! aglow in light flowing outside in the cold from the windoes within! Grignr wonederred if the warm had also bekkoned forthwith the chance of whine and women? He would so offer welcome oppertunity of playfull exorcise for his loins, in which the cold had so ungorged his manlyhood. So guided by his lust did Grignr hasten to the stabeles beside the inn. His horse steed was happy with glee also at the site of mares in the stable; and quickley hastened to mount them all as Grignr marched to the indoor with his arder driven foot steps.

The door opened and Grignr stepped threw and looked to where he might see a wench. And the wench looked up the besodded traveler she was giving rich attenshun too. She gasped in buetifully breathing breadth at Grignr and stood up quickly. The besodded travalers head banged on the stone with the back of his head. She walk to Grignr, her breasts catapulting in front of her as too pointed globules of sex goo. And so it came to be that Grignr was getting warm!

"You mighty man of a warrior?" SHe lustifullously gasped in lust. Grignr looked at her face and noticed in keen site it had two eyes and a nose and a mouth that drooled desire. There was hair on her head too.

'Woold that you would bed me on this floor! Now!" she projectfully beggered him.

Grignr laughed lowdly and kissed her mouth on the lips as he did so, then pusht her from him in a surprised shove of playful banter.

"Aye, wench! I shalt bed thou soon!! But!! I have been jerneyed three days now since my horse dyed and the coldness is cold in my sinnews and bones and manlyness. Haste! bring wine for to heat my blood that I drink to my health and you service you're King. For Behold! I am King Grignr!"

The woman then cryed in happy tears and other wenches, all with many girly parts of their bodies came and cryed to in joy of seeing there King! And hopin he would have his wya with them at once.

But there remaned a female who did'nt not drool and crye. She looked at him in mean eyes that were thoughtful with ideas in her brain. Then she made smile at him and laughed in tone.

"Do thou not remeber me, Oh! King?' she stated with lots of unbeleif in her voice. I am Carthena, whom didst be saveed by thou and didst adventured with in many dark tunnles 'neath the Norgolian empire! It was I were with you when from those carvans that you bought fourth the Eye of Argon!!!!!!!"

Grinr stared at Carthena's gasping brests on her chest that heaved in poignint fortitude and then he rembered. He pushed over the wench to the floor, giving her and the all wenches a look that promsed there pleasure would be sated many times many. He delicatly strode to Carhena kissed her mouth on her lips, angered love getting them enough to melt water.

"Aye, aye remmeber, female! and my lips two score more!" he exclaimed while he kept his mouth on her lips so she coold no prostest. He threw his head. Back then laughed. "Be ye the first female of the wenches here? Verily, if it be ye, I shall warm my lusty loins under my cloth with you first so that my testicles wilt weep joyfuly."

"Neigh, King Grignr," said she, 'but it has come to pass that this inn blongs to me of my ownship.' Now she laughed, making her nipples giggle with fortuitous vibrations. "Thou art housed in my inn!" And then Grignr gasped. "you weer ment to cometh on this day, O my! King!"

They rushed to the backroom in the back eeger to disgust the matter and got there so Carthena started the torch and then lit the candel sitting on the table with it so light explded into all the corners or the backromm while Grignr smiled at the rumbling beauty of the females sweaty butt before recalling to his mine's memry he was destined for a vast mission which glowered be yonder his sight in the distant dark.

The female Carthena took out a stone tabelt from the wall adn .unrolled it on the table placed itt on."Behold1 King Grignr! the sacrid words of Jarbinx!!' Cartha wisperred softly as she unrolled the sacrid words that lie on the table. "In these sacrid words are your destiny lies!"

"Spek the words to your King," Grignr growlerfly barked. "My loins and sinnews most ashrewdly crave for battel!"

"And it is battle you cravings shall have! For Jarbinx converses planely on stone that you shall slay a dragon but not any dragon but a dragon who is King of dragons and is your mortar enemy and whose name beith known to ye as Drignr the Dragon!"

Chapter 1½

Steed Horse of Grignr plowed threw the cold snow in verilly the same astounding manner he had plowed threw the mares at the Inn! Grignr opent his cold eyes to stare into the blinding snow of blanked out cold whiteyness that betrayed no site of naught but cold snow. Three leagues away before him layed the Hjrezarnorklinianmy mountain—it's sharp edges of outline clear as the burnig fule of outraguous anger and indigination in Grignr's heart which heated him and Steed Horse in the very cold.

For behold! It was Drignr who made Grignr put on the barbarian path on the night the dragon swoooped over the village of his ancestors and burned all but Grignr in more than three bursts of furryous crispy vengince and firy dragon breath. All was gone? Grignr hated Drignr, more then any thing, living, or dead. And now, Grignr vowed with all he's heart he—Grignr no less! —would cut off the head of Drignr the Dragon and baste in the glory of the deed of deheading the head!!!

It was many ours later and dark had fallen and brought more cold when Grignr arriveded succussfully and with garganguin success at the base of Hjrezarnorklinianmy mountain, upon which a missive stoned doors a hundred feet hi into the mountain was truthfully all that lie between Grignr and his justfully smoky revenge. For Drignr was beyond those doors and deepin in his lyre, awaiting his certain doom, though the dragons mind did not yet see it in his brain vision. Grinr laughed at the thinking of the sticky humor of the site of Drign'rs eye when at last he saw his ubiquitous doom.

Leaving his steed horse behind to contemplate his master's revenge on a four legged beast such as he, Grignr pushed open the a door and entered the darkly, dankly, smelly, cave. The cave's ceiling was so high as to be unseeble in the darkness? Or so Grignr thought as.

Striding with mighty stride, and his swoard drawed ably in his right hand of human might and resolute, Grignr strode across the cabern floor until it was thirtyone minutes and fourty seconds later when LO! he reacht the tunnel that lurched down into the darkness as Drignr's soul to the Layer of Drignr the Dragon! Giving out a shamefuless bellow of guffaws, Grinr descented down the tunnel. Far off and down, he could see and hear Drignr's fire and gas.

"THOU HAST COME TO DISPATH ME, WEEK MORTAL!??!!?!" BELlowed Drignr when Grignr was still a longly way saway. "THEN BE IT A FOOL WHO APROCHES ME TO MEET A CRISPY AND TASTEY DEATH!!! COME FORWORD THEN, FOOD!!!! FOR I AM DRIGNR THE DRAGON, YOUR EATER!!!!" Bellowed Drigner when Grignr was still a lonlgy away.

Grignr guffawed and chortled with dire voice and pulled his sword from it's scabberd. His sweaty skin flikered in the heat and sweated in the light. His eyes blazed forth in sparkling glistening of virile hate even as his loins poured forth in it's maleness and might of strengthened sinnews of mighty legs. BEHOLD the prefection of all men and women, too!

"You art the one so doomed to die this day, Drignr! For twenty years and a fortnight have I sought to undo thy head from thy neck and shoulders and body and today that day hath come!" Grignr preferred his sword to that it's gleaming steel!! "I am Grignr the King now, but long ago I were but a boy and you destroyed all that I loved and I oathed rebenge upon thee most bad dragon. This day is how you shall pay!"

And uttering these word didst Grignr draw his steel sword and charge the evile creature who stood fourty feet high and sixtyseven feet long and with a wing span os fiftyone feet, though he didn't weigh as much so he could still fly. Even Drignr's head was awesomely huge being nearly sixteen feet long from ears to fire belching snout!

But now! an error?? was mead bye the awfull and wicked dragon! For LO! tho he twer able to fly alauoght and burn down fire on the brave and charging Grignr, the ceiling of the lyre wert to low to fly, being only thrity feet and twelfh handspans but in height!!!

Seing and identifying his error in wrathful stupidity, Drignr roared his rage and threw up fire on Grignr. But Grignr rolled and rolled out of the way until it came to pass that verity he was right by next to Drignr's clawed foot and then Drignr threw up more fire but Grignr rolled away to the back end of where Drignr kept his tail and and he tittered delitfully as Drignr didst burst flame even upon his own foot!!! And he roared in hurt!

Grignr viewed his only chance to defeat a mighty foe! With nibbleness that many songs would records for sentries, Grignr raced up the tale and alongside the spine of Drignr's back to the ribs! The shoulder blades!! The neck!!! THE HEAD OF DRIGNER!!!! And with mightily justly strengthy ardor didst Grigner strike! Again! and again again!! The head was nearly off the neck when Drignr cried. "THO HAST BESTED ME WITH HONOR, GRIGNR!!! I BOW TO YOU AND YOU"RE MIGHTY SWORD WHICH IS EVEN NOW SEVERING MY HUGE HEAD!!!" And with that final roar, Drignr's head fell down from his neck and give a loud plog on the floor... dead like the rest of Drignrs headless body.

The cavern rumbled! Only in that minute of victry didst Grignr understand in his head that it was Drignr's hate and evile and anger, and sick sole that kept Mount Hjrezarnorklinianmy. For then Grinr undertsood and remmebere that Hjrezarnorklinianmy mean 'the dragons anger and pithy vengince shalt be wrout in firely bile"!!

Grignr had broad urgency to flee atonce and did so. He stuffed the Drigner's head into a sack around Grignr's waist, then shoved gold coins from the fourty food piles of gold coins Drignr didn't loftily collect in evel greed most foulest! Then Grignr left!!!

He dashed out to horse steed and mounted him from behind before racing into the cold night, where the coldness was now less cold as the Drignr's warm blood soaked threw the sack and warmed both hores stted and the magnificently viactoriously warrior as they roded back to the inne

Chapter Two

When Grignr returned to the inn, he let horse steed into the stables to celebrat his victorious master's deed by having many more victries with the maers evan as Grignr did the same thing in the inn for witch he earned.

Leave Drignr's head outside the dorr for it was too huge to enter the inne, Grignr opened the door to enter the inn.

All became quiet from their noice and fivroloty at the entrance of Grignr. And Carthena saw the blood all over Grignr's close and knew deep, deep, inside her interior, Grignr had slayed Drignr the Dragon!! She panted with eager rewards promised and her breasts heaved in super sexy breath and she gasped and fell to the floor to bow. And all the females and men also fell down too and there breasts also were super sexy and they gasped out in one single voice:

LONG LEAVE THE KING!!

Grignr in the Land of Er-Urz
Ian Randal Strock

The muscle-bound Ecordian came across a cadre of prostitutes who had spent the night singing lustfully, and as a consequence, the whores were hoarse. But they would not due to carry Grignr onward. Neither wood the ability to construct him a vessel to sale the reever through these lands.

"What you need," cried the narrator, "is a mighty weapon!"

"Quill I find it nearby?" beseeched the breach-clouted clod.

"Mightier than that petty blade you carry, seek in the animal enclosure. There you will find the pen, which is indeed mightier than the flown bird."

"Flown bird? Soared?"

"Aye, there's the cub. This device, called 'editor,' can set you to rites."

"Gods have nought to do—"

"Take it, take it!" screamed the long-suffering audience.

Shruffing his showeders, Grignr took the pen of correction, and felt grate power coarsing threw hymn.

"With this, I will be the master of all I sorbet. I will reed and rite, and possibly even rithmetic, as we travail two the three-lined hell sides of yon mondegreen verdant… Wait!" yelled he who was strong like a bull and smart like a tractor—"even eye ken sea this cursed tulle is knot—"

The narrator's laughter cut Grignr off mid-malapropism.

"Your pardon, grated one," wheezed the narrator. "You have taken up the typo maker, not the typo braker. But as shadows are not seen without light, nor good recognized in the absence of evil, the fixer can only be found with the maker. As thou travelest the Fleetest of Streets, passed the Grayest of Ladies, toward the Stiles of Manualism, seek that which seekst that which you carry, and all shall be as blew penciled."

Muddering under his braeth at the horrer thus inflicted upon himself—knot to menshun his long-suffering readers—Grignr took the maker of typographic Er-urz, smote the narrator, and took his leave of the hoarse horseless whores.

This, thought Grignr, is what I get for destroying the idle in Chapter 6 of the original story.

As the sun descended into the crimson west, the gathering darkness made it too difficult for the narrator to follow the action....

– 1 ½ –

It was night, too dark to see the page clearly enough to continue writing the story. And so, the narrator did not.

– 2 –

After the long night of terrible travails—thankfully illegible to the poor readers do to the dark—a new day dawned, giving the narrator leave to continue telling the tall tail.

As Grignr reached the trees, he considered the wood about him. Riding all through the night and the rising dawn on the sway-backed horse he had acquired through the incredible deeds of derring-did which remain invisible in Chapter 1 ½, Grignr ached of the road. Perhaps, thought he, I can use some of this lumbar for a little lumber support.

If only he cud klew in on his indeterminate destination, the location of the typo braker, to cleanse his pallet and the readers's reeding materiel.

Unfortunately, an easy solution did not present itself, and the narrator knew Grignr was to remain part of the precipitant. Grignr, of course, did not understand the pun, nor did he understand the concept of a precipitants and solutions.

At any rate, Grignr continued his journey, occasionally looking at the typo maker the narrator had gifted him in Chapter 1. The maker, for its part, quivered eagerly in the direction of its counterpart, leading Grignr ever onward, ever upward, ever ward.

– 3 –

Thus it was, after many long traverses, that Gringr found his way to the editorial office of the great and mighty publisher, the one—blessed be he—who might indeed no the weigh to correct the text, and save the readers.

"Stand, dog," snarled the savage Accordion. "Long have I traveled, far have I ventured, that I mite at this anointed our make good on the please of our reeders, to be able to find there weigh threw the horrid spelling of which I, personally, no knot.

"Wherefore, there [the narrator interjects to note that the proper phrasing should, 'Therefore, where…', though he fears it's a losing cause to seek proper spelling or phrasing at this point] have you hidden this marvelous tool, this maker of cents?"

Standing, the editor reached into his pocket protector—fairly bursting with pens, pencils, and other such writing implements—and pulled forth a magically glowing blue pencil.

"This, noble knight, this is that which you seek. The blue pencil of correction, long eschewed by the larger publishers seeking to save a buck. With it, your horrible misspellings and awkward utterances will be a thing of the past. Clarity will reign, and your readers shall know the joy of enjoying your story."

"Give it to me!" screamed Grignr! "Let me dew what I may."

"There is but one problem, Grinder," said the editor. "One that I fear will continue to plague us for an endless time."

Gringr felt the swaet braeming on his brow.

"In this land, no one has yet invented the pencil sharpener."

Grignr unleashed his sword, slew the editor, and declared the absurdity at…

An End.

God Quest
Genevieve Iseult Eldredge

The frozen ice rimed path protuberated upwards like
the ridged mailen fist of Mrifk, up through the freezing
cold climbs of snow thrushed peeks, whence the thin air
currents blazed in the nostrils like twinn bonfires and tore
rampantly at the quivering bowles.

Moonlight sprinkled in a descending motion on the
grism, deathly environs, casting its lumescent rays across
the drift crusted earth. The shadow chocked sky screed
with charcoal black flocks of aggrieved carrion birds
sporting blood red eyes and flesh shrouding their gnarly
beaks, stirred from their visceral feast.

Not even the most viscuous of beasts and legionniers
dared aquest the baren lands of these timeless snowy
wastes.

Only barbarians and gods.

Sleeped in the frigid northern summits whents all his
savage people affronted from, Grignr tossed aside his
shaggy red mein and leashed his mount onward to the
snow swirled mountaintop. His mighty glittering trews
and thighs flexed around the beaten leather saddle,
keeping the plunging crimsoned nostrilled beast in play,
lest a sudden sideways shunt toss them off the mountain
into the hell-pits of stygia.

Ahead, squalidly, the legendary taven of the gods
secreted in the mountains appeared as if combing into view
for the very first time. The hoary mists of time perforated,
and the four-story chateau loosed its grantite visage on the

unsuspecting barbarian protruding from a dingy crossroads betwixt four slinking alleys permeated with fetid snow and the stinking rummage of an ages-old battle.

Espying the hostelry with his blaxing emerald green orbs, Grignr felt his carmelized blood begin to once more percolate and ignite with the lustful premise of battle with a god.

Tying up his foamy stead, Grigrn ascended toward the tavern's porch area.

Kikcing the thick oaken rimed door open, the warious titan servied the groups of thives, pirates, and other nonprominent cuuthroats clustered around beaten tables guzzling cheap ale from thick oaken mugs and bickering beneath their breaths in a stealthy shadow cant.

Dice ratted and darts pierced as the sneering cutthroats plied their swily games of luck and hustle. Willing women with outcropped brests sat on laps, smothering inflamed faces with rubish beknighted lips as the cutthroats cupped their consenting busts.

Other mangly groups maligned themselves about the tavern's dusky interiors. Shifty eyes and other various sight organs slithered with hellacious greediness over the chisled barbarians finely honed gem encrusted broad sword. Grignr booted a stray tentacle off his thick leather sandal and cupped the door closed.

Over the mess, the minstrels ripped a jiggedy promenade.

The largish round great room was dimely lit by intermittent torch light and greasy, oblique candles. The place reeked of cruddy ale plush with dark shadows and dim hideouts thick with theives and assassins waiting for the right patsy to tounce upon unawares.

There were no gods anywhere, that Grignr's keen panther like emeralds could discern.

Striding to a stout oaken table, a morrow emotion seized the huge Ecordian in its grips. He lived to give vent to his lusty fury in the heats of battle. His blood broiled to sweave his sword through the skulls of his gibbering enemiies and sprawl them agonizedly to the rotting aperture of their bony final graves.

But alas, weaks of lazing on the throne had nummed his buttocks and robbed his once keen instincts and animal senses down to small nubs.

Hardened by harsh weathers and the steel of the sword, battle was the life gust in Grignr's grinding lungs, and no mere calvalry against mortal men would wet his appiesement for glory and the spils of victory.

He needed the bloody adversage of godly combat. But none were in residents.

Quaffing up a nearby tankard that was sorely unattended in his crushing mitt, Grignr guzzled the testy brew running down his surly chin.

A steel shod blade smacked the cup away from Grignr's forcible hand and golden yellow flotsam and jetsons sprinkled the area in a reak foul swirl.

"You shall rue stealing a soldier of Crin's ale? Die, Ecordian dog!" the soldier ejasculated with a sneer twisting his mocking countenance.

The knowing gleam of death grimmed Grignr's eye sockets as he reaved his mighty blade from its jewel leather casing.

The soldier, who had followed Grignr's frost bitten tracks all the way from Crin busied himself by reaching for his flanked blade, but quickly found to his dismay that he had not accurately calculated the confines of the frumious barbarian's inflamed reach.

With a nauseating sicken, Grignr's blade scortched in a slivered flash groving deep into the soldier's nude gullet lopping off his head.

A gooey spout of blood oodled from the offensive oval and the hapless soldier crimped over his eyes like glass marbles seeing only the stygian darkness of nonexistence.

Grignr's knife-like orbs told him that dead soldier had not ventured on this foolhardy quest alone. Others of his fellows came thrsuting up from their chairs, reaping their wicked cressets from boned scabbards gleaming in the greasy torch light emanately glowing from the bar.

They wore twisted leather head bands transfixed with fauceted red rubies in the centers. Attiring their torsos were brownhided hauberks that came halfway down their thighs with silver meshed braided girdles and high soft boots enshrouding their bare feet. Brackish steel languished in their tightly corded fists, catching the darkened flashing of the torches scatterpated around the saloon.

The foul soldiery of Crin meant to sack the husky reward some faithless cackling nobly had leveraged upon his head.

Barking aside the table, Grignr leaped, naked save for a loin cloth and g-string wearing an iron helmet pronged with steel and rude leather sandals enmeshing his feet.

Shaking his shaggy, robust mane, he ejaculated a fearful roar.

"Know when you face your betters, sluts" ! bellowed Grignr, lustily spining to face the many, furious soldiers of Crin now speaing up from their tables.

Dashing forthwith a forward looping cleft, Grignr expressly sliced the brains of the harried soldier before him, pureeing his splattered brains into a misting death cocktail.

"You will pay for that with your life blood, cur" scramed the second soldier. His eyes were wide as he percepted his fellow in an egg huddled mess on the beer-stoked floor, eviscerating in agony.

Before they could loose their weapons, Grignr lithly braised through their rank. His sword twirled like a whirly gig of doom, his red hair flowing in the wind breezes as his blood flocked blade segmented his foes from their last breaths of life and their escaping life fluids sprinkled the stoneage.

The remains of the patronry sequestered in the tavern gasped in shock and aww gaping with their mouths open in perplexity as the giant titan perseverated the soldiers, fleeing them to the shallow fusky tomes of their forbears.

The door bonged open. Another falinx of soldiers crammed their armor shod breastplates in through the doorward, bustling at the grieved barbarian to mellow him in a blood searing trap of iron spears.

Enthused, Grignr swlved and razed his mighty xcleaving sword over his head, his trews pulsing and swole, and prepped a thunderous overhead blaze, but before he could leash the sweeping, burning cleft upon the inflamed Crin soldiers, a nother warrior butted him in the sides.

"Apologies, my large friend, but leave some for the rest of us."

Chapter 1 ½

The newcomber was encased in a peech gerkin encirculated by a thin golden braided belt and a matching cresset halfway up his forehead. Sandals twined up his calves, tied with golden threads and his bulky corded pect muscles rippled and swayed toughly in the lusty wind.

His shock of whitish hair stood on ends, and streamed out longer than Grigrn's who obeying the feral Laws of his wilderness bred people had nust clipped his twines since taking up the steel.

Cleaving a hammer that seizured with lightning, the magjestic blonde warrior swept the roomwith his rampant heaving forearms, bashing Grignr's foes senseless with thunderas clefts of his writhing hammer sizzling their flesh down to gibbering insensate puddles.

Whence the dust and dinge cleared, Grignr reconned the weltering warrior gobbeted in the crimson rubish blood of the soldiers enswirled on the crimsoned flag stones.

The new flexed his lashing muscles. "What say you to a challenge, barbarian?"

Chapter 2

Grignr steepled in his juices, every muscle enfired, sauch raging heated blood fueled by a life of grinding steel and furious battle could not turn away any challenge.

Swilveling to face the other, Grigrn roved his massive two hander sword around his skull and perfigurated three times around his nuggety form.

"Prepare to feast apon the broadside of my blade, rapscallion" shouted Grignr!

Finally leasing the vortexed cleft he had held over his fiery tress, the vigoruos titan smote his wrath down on his steely foe, releasing a piercing rigged war cry from his grinding throat. But the hammer smitted upward, meeting the barbarian's rippling sword loudly clashing and throwing both gigantic men backward.

The other warrior's icy blue sapphires burned into Grignr's jade green ones and he ejaculated a fierce battle cree as he crested the hammer.

Lightning crashed inside the tavern, but Grignr dodged to one side by lifting one foot and then the other, dancing aside as the forks of searing passed under his arm. Throwing his weight foward, he rolled and came up to one knee, sweeping his sword upso fast his besotted opponent could not repost the blood thirsting iron seeking to drink deeply of his beating jugglar.

"No man can defeat the likes of me!" Mans zealous forearm attentuated forward. The hammer obstusively struck aagain, and Grignr's sword clattered harmlessly off the eeriely, glowering metal.

Grign circled around his opponent pacing around him with quick semicircular steps. Perplexed, his gristly brows knitted together furvishly.

Never had the feisty Ecordian faced his equal. Never had his wild barbarous blood boiled so effervescently. The gripping desire to clash blades again sent him sailing over the brinks of sanity.

Scowling a confident ulation, Grignr leaped at his mercurial dodging foe, clasping his nefarious arms around the tree trunk waist before the other warrior could dance off freely. The two wrestled back and forth, potent colossuses heaving and grunting with the extreme thriving of their efforts.

The tavern rocked and quivered like a bowful of jelly. The minstrels scoffed up a lively jig.

Energetic hours passed but neither steely muscled combatant would surfeit. Sweat grimed their questing shoulder blades and dripped from their surly brows and the tavern resounded with their mighty pancreation.

Finally cleaving stealth to the sward, Grignr appraised his foe and turned the advantage over him. Slipping free, he cleaved overhead a blazr of furious smoking steel that loped the brand warrior's left arm clean off and knocked him sundering into the wall.

The patronry gawped openly swirled in their fine raimints and several coins surruptishly exchanged greedy hands.

In a victor's triumph, Grignr loomed over his vanquished foe, his glaze incandescent and his lively blood singing after such a bloody medley of steel.

Surprise and shock grippled him tautly as the other warrior abruptly stood up, hale and refreshed. A new arm had revamped the one Grignr had lopped off, looking even more puissant and capable in its stolid musculature.

Bewilderment rushed in Grignr's ears. "What is your calling stranger?" he queried? from behind the cross pommel of his sword.

"Thor, god of thunder, though some know me by less obtuse names." Thor held forth a hand capped in sturdy fingers. "Come, friend, let us slake our lips on honeywine in cebration of your glorious victory, and your ascension to the radiance halls of immortality."

Grignr waxed stoic but his innards feinted over the nefarious inflations of the stunning god's arresting claim. To be given throng among the halls of the gods his forefathers would have prided him greatly.

Thor crasped Grignr on the back and swilved the surprise pondering barbarian around to face what was a sudden tavern teaming in stalwart heroes and scoundrels of woebegone days of yore. Attired in silver and gold tonics, sparkling enameled shields and cresset blades and coronated in glistering tiaras they were indeed deities of many variegated hails.

"Defeat a god and you become one." Thor laughed ironicacially!

A stacky horned god slapped a beer into Grignr's stunned and vice-like fist and with a slovering bleat tooted off. A damb broke, and the burled giant found himself suddenly warmly and well-receivedly encompassed by gods of every staid greeting him as an equal and embracing him brotherly.

Grignr's heart sang a mustre of battle as their words tripped on his ears. "Welcome home, Grignr. Barbarian. King. God."

Grignr's Swift Sword of Vengeance
Daniel M. Kimmel

Grignr had trod for countless miles. His steed had long ago breathed its last breath. Grignr had managed to turn the carcass into a pouch of coins at a rendering plant whereby it had conveniently died, but Carthena turned out to be a faithless wench. He awakened after a night of ribald revelries to discover both she and the coins were long gone. She had even taken the pouch.

He needed a sponsor, some liege under whose aegis he could return to the field of battle for more feats of derring-do. Leaving his fate to the Fates, he chose a path at random and began his new journey.

As the sun rose to scalding heat in the Noonday sky, he espied a farm where a spindly looking crone was attempting to cajole a reluctant oxen to pull a plow across her field. He leaned against the railing of the wooden fence and shouted, "Ho, crone! I have not eaten in days."

"Begone, beggar," she hissed, revealing a few remaining teeth.

Grignr pulled himself erect, allowing the sunlight to glisten over his sweat-slicked musculature. "No beggar am I," he replied. "Would you share your humble victuals with a wandering soul if I first plowed your field?"

The woman glanced at the oxen who was now rooting in the dirt for a leftover turnip from the prior crop. She looked over at the impressive warrior and considered his offer. "In truth, my farm has fallen on hard times since my husband was trampled to death by a flock of sheep a fortnight ago. If you can truly get this oxen to ply his trade, I'll gladly share some fresh mutton with you."

In a single bound Grignr hopped the fence railing, deftly planting his sandaled feet on the other side. "I have no need for the services of this beast," he said, unhitching it from the plow. "Go prepare our feast, such as it is, while I endeavor to plow your field." With that he began shoving the agricultural device in geometric furrows up and down the field.

After lunch, in which the crone shared that it brought another of her late husband's murderers to justice, she inquired whether Grignr would like to stay on.

"Thank thee, fair crone," said the satiated Grignr, "but I am a fabled warrior and need to offer my services to someone of noble birth. Can you point me in the right direction?"

The disappointed widow expressed the hope that mayhaps Grignr could return at harvest time. Until then, she indicated with a wave of a gristle-covered bone which was the route that would take him to the big city where he might find his fortune. She insisted that he first take advantage of her by taking a hot bath. "It would not be meet to arrive covered with the dust of the road and the field."

Grignr agreed and was soon nakedly soaking in a tub of hot and soapy water. While the crone fetched more hot water and admired the attributes of her manly guest, Grignr mused on what the widow looked like in her youth. "She must have been a comely lass, instead of the old hag she is now. Why she must be 30 years of age if she's a day."

Now as bathed as he had been in many a year and newly dressed—she had even washed his loincloth—Grignr offered a profusion of thanks to his hostess and took his leave, hoping to reach the nearby city by nightfall.

It was dusk when he arrived, and he had no idea where to get his bearings or find his future sponsor. Towering buildings surrounded him, strangely clad people stared at him but gave him wide berth. Indeed, it was berth so wide he could not even ask them where he was or how he might proceed. Starting to despair he was startled out of his reverie by a shout, "Hail fellow warrior."

Grignr turned to see a man dressed much as he, swinging an impressive halberd. Grignr put his hand on his sword, ready to defend himself from attack, but the man was smiling. "Great cosplay, man," the stranger said, "I guess you're heading to the con."

Grignr recognized some of the words the man used, but much was gibberish to his ears. The stranger held his halberd at his left side and held out his right hand. "Name's Bruce. Let's head over to the hotel." Grignr allowed the man to briefly grasp his hand and then followed him to an immense castle which he was told was known as the Share-a-ton. Obviously the nobleman there had accumulated great wealth, and Grignr was eager to see if the lord would find Grignr someone with whom he might share.

Immediately inside the structure was a huge space that both dazzled and baffled the warrior, but Bruce led him to a table in an area that was immediately recognizable. "Two ales!!!" shouted Bruce to a passing wench, and presently two large glasses filled with amber beverage were brought to the table.

"It's on me," Bruce continued in a friendly manner. "It's not often I see such craftsmanship in a costume. Did you do it yourself?"

Grignr happily swallowed half the glass and then responded, "Do what myself?"

"Your outfit. Did you make it yourself or did you have help?"

"I killed, skinned and tanned the hides but they were finished by others."

"Impressive," said Bruce, rising. "I have to get to a panel. Perhaps I'll catch you at one of parties later." He left some paper on the table which he said would pay for the ale and took his leave.

Now Grignr had time to look around. He saw many people crowding in one area and figured someone might be able to direct him to the lord of the castle. He saw three young women who wore maybe three yards of silky material between them and followed them into what proved to be a tiny room.

"What floor?" one of them queried before fully taking in the mighty warrior. "Nice loincloth," she added, giggling.

"It is freshly washed."

"I bet it is." And she giggled again. Suddenly the entrance to the room closed and it seemed to be moving.

"What magic is this?"

This led all three of the wenches to more laughter. The oldest looking one—she must have been at least 20—deflected his question and asked, "Who are you supposed to be?"

Striking a pose that had sent his enemies fleeing and rendered women helpless he announced, "I am Grignr!"

"The Barbarian?" asked the middle one who had heretofore been silent. "You should be going to the Eye of Argon."

Grignr stiffened. "The Eye of Argon is here? But I saw it destroyed with my own eyes. Where in this castle has it reappeared?"

The eldest pulled out some sort of scroll and said, "It just started in the Theis Conference Room on the second floor." She pressed a button in an array to the right of the entrance to the room. "We're getting off here. Come to our party in room 2323 later. You've got plenty of time to go to Eye of Argon while we set up." The entrance magically opened and the three wenches departed.

Grignr was too startled to respond, and the door closed again. The room began to descend and Grignr wondered what foul magic was involved when the door opened again and a bodiless voice announced, "Second Floor—Conference Rooms."

Grignr stepped out of the room to find a hallway filled with people in all varieties of garb, only some of which made sense. Fate smiled on the mighty warrior as Bruce emerged from the mass. "Friend Bruce," hailed Grignr, "Where can I find the Eye of Argon?"

"I'm heading that way myself," he said. "I'm hoping I can get through an entire page."

Bruce and Grignr entered a room that was filled to capacity. It took him several moments to understand was happening. At the front of the room, people were struggling to read from some parchments while other people in the room roared with laughter.

"Remove yourself Sirrah, the wench belongs to me;"
Blabbered a drunken soldier, too far consumed by the
influences of his virile brew to take note of the superior
size of his adversary.

Grignrlithly bounded from the startled female, his
face lit up to an ashen red ferocity, and eyes locked in a
searing feral blaze toward the swaying soldier.

"To hell with you, braggard!" Bellowed the angered
Ecordian, as he hefted his finely honed broad sword.

The people in the room laugh and cheered. They
were laughing at Grignr. They were mocking him. They
were ridiculing the horrible ordeal he had endured. At
first he sat there stunned. But when some of the people
began miming his tortures, he could bear the calumny no
further.

"Stop," he shouted, rising from his seat and drawing
his sword. "I am Grignr, who slew Agaphim and
destroyed the idol of Argon. This is not a source of
mockery but of tragedy."

This brought new laughter. "Wait your turn,
Barbarian," taunted the person presently reading the
scrolls, to a new round of applause.

Grignr's blood ran hot as strode through the crowd to
the front of the room and slew the servant of Argon.
Waving the now bloodied sword he turned to the
audience, "Who next wants to meet my blade?"

Some screamed and rushed to the doors to flee while
some foolishly thought the Grignr of reality only bore
some resemblance to the Grignr they had found a figure
of amusement. Their blood was soon mingled in the
fibers of the tawdry carpet blanketing the room. Two new
arrivals claimed they were "Security" and Grignr

demanded they secure the room for him. Instead they attacked him and soon met the same fate as the others.

Finally the only living beings in the room were Grignr and Bruce. "Will you also mock me?" demanded Grignr. "If so, prepare to meet thy doom."

Bruce raised his hands. "No way, man. I'm impressed with how far you're willing to go to stay in character, but I think you better leave while the getting is good."

Grignr allowed himself a sigh and then returned his sword to its scabbard. "Thank you, friend. Your many kindnesses will not be forgotten." With that Grignr, flecked with blood from his fallen foes, found his way out of the Share-a-ton and to the road that had brought him there.

"Yo, crone!!"

The elderly hag looked up. "As I live and breathe. Grignr, have you returned?"

"I have indeed. Are you still looking for someone who can plow your field and reap your crops?"

"Indeed I am," she allowed.

"Then I am your man," said Grignr, who decided that 30 wasn't so old after all.

Ounna's Rock
Jean Marie Ward

The smoking tavern churned with meaty, unwashed bodies, lip-smacking noises, and shouts for more ale. Leaning back on his stool, the russet-haired northern barbarian Grigner pressed the hardy muscles of his bronze-burnished back against the greasy wall and waggled his eyebrows prevarcatively at the licksome dancer weaving among the crowd.

A fat, bearded captain of the Schist city watch grabbed the dancer's wrist and hauled her into his lap. Eager to win her favors but lacking the gold to buy them, Grignr readied himself to leap to her defense. The wench swatted the watchman's helm sideways. Roaring with laughter, the captain released her. She bounded to her swaying feet and jiggled the coins sewn to her slitted skirt.

Grignr dropped back onto his stool and morosely took another swig of the house's thin ale. The coin-bedazzened dancer flitted from one moneyed patron to another without sparing him a single glance. To be skint in the city of Schist was indeed a sorry state of affairs. Even a man as tall, lusty, and well-made as the emerald-eyed Ecordian slept alone—assuming he could find a place to sleep at all.

The young barbarian had hoped to make a name forhimself in Schist. The city was as rich as any along the Soutran Coast but presented few opportunities for a foreign-born thief. All its criminal enterprises—including the fences essential to profiting from one's pilfering—

were controlled by nepotistic local gangs who only employed their relatives. If his luck didn't change soon, he'd be forced to hire on as a mercenary in the service of some puliing aristocrat.

A slim, cloaked figure slid in front of his table, interrupting his dark musings. "Shall I read your future, noble sir?"

A flash of scentillant sapphirine eyes and pale orchidine flesh peeped from beneath the folds of her hood. Grigner blinked. The voluminous garment shrouding her form was tattered and patched, teasing his eyes with tantalizing glimpses of the shapely limbs and blooming flesh beneath. Stripped of her rags, this maid might prove comelier than the other. Perhaps he need not sleep alone this night. "Are you fortune teller, lass?"

Pearalescent white fingers peeled the hood back from a heart-shaped face with pouting, cherry-pursed lips. "I am more than that. Your hand, sirrah."

She was a saucy wench for one so small. Grignr extended his hand. It took both of hers to hold it. Cool fingers slivered across his calloused pam. "I see a kingdom in your future."

He shrugged and casually booted aside a pair of drunks whose flailing fight threatened to upend his table. "The future is a long way off."

"It may be nearer than you think." She leaned over the wobbly table. He winy breath tickled his ear. "Have you ever heard of Ounnas Rock?"

He hefted his tankard in one hand and drew her closer with the other. "No."

She smiled the smile of sirens across the ages who know they have intrigued a man's interest. "It stands in the heart of a cave within the walls of the royal cemetery, guarded by the prince's strongest warriors. Held fast in the stone is a jeweled handled sword of the finest watered steel. Only the bravest of men can draw it from the rock's implacable gripe. But the prize is worth the toil, for whomever wields the sword in battle cannot be defeated and will one day wear a crown."

"If that be true, why hasn't someone pulled it free 'ere now?"

Her ample bosom heaved as she shrugged. "Mayhap they fear the guards, or the terrors rumored to lie beyond the cemetery's gate. I have heard reports that the princes of Schist perform dark sorceries among the graves. Does that frighten you? Have the times become so decadent that an Ecordian is afraid of a little magic?" she flirted.

His hand slid down her back to the tight globblar swells of her hips. "No more than I fear Schist's soldiers. These southern folk are feeble swordsmen."

"Indeed," she concurred, "not one of them would meet me by the cemetery gates at midnight."

She slipped like water from his grasp and melted into the crowd. All that was left was the memory of her words and her secret smile.

- **2** -

The minx was easy on the eyes, and with his purse flatter than a downward-facing flounder, Grignr felt compelled to investigate her tale. Even without the whiff of destiny, a jeweled blade and golden gates were sure to fetch a high price. If he couldn't find a local buyer, so be it. Schist was hardly the only market on the coast.

But desperate as he was for funds, he wasn't so far gone he couldn't smell a rat. Something was amiss here. There were plenty of native bravos big enough and ambitious enough to take up her challenge, soldiers and sorcery be damned. Why cast her lures at an outlander?

Wary of treachery, he armed himself accordingly and arrived a full hour early to their rendezvous. Rumors of magic and monsters concerned him less than human agendas. Decapitation was a sovereign cure for enchanters and eldritch horrors alike.

The cemetery lay at the base of Palace Hill, snugged against the sheer east side of the massif. From his vantage in the inky shadow of the nearby temple of Kalla, Grignr failed to detect any openings in the rock, but it should be easy enough to find once he got past the graveyard's high stone wall.

Two burly guards flanked the cemetery's only entrance, a locked iron gate that faced the street. Another six patrolled the remainder of the wall, which added some credit to the seer's tale. There must be something of value here. Why else would the prince pay soldiers to guard the dead? Grignr's size and speed made him a peerless bawler, but he saw no reason to fight when stealth would serve. There was always the (admittedly slight) chance a soldier could escape and raise the alarm. If there had been trees or buildings overlooking the wall, he would have entered that way. Since there were none, he needed to know the timing of the soldiers rounds, when and where they turned away. While he watched, he readied the tools he brought with him.

As he finished securing the knot on his grappling hook, his keen senses detected the approach of stealthy footpads. He oozed deeper into the tenebrous gloom. A flowery fragrance struck his nose. He swerved. His hands grasped a bundle of cloth, curves... and sticks? He dragged captive into the moonlight.

The short pallod face regarded him blandly. "You didn't trust me." She sounded more amused than surprised. She lifted a pair of unlit brands for his inspection. "I have brought torches blessed by the holy nuns of Kalla and flint to light them."

"Why?" he frowned. "The wall is well lit, and torches won't be much use against the guards."

"They aren't for the guards. They're fo after we scale the wall." She pointed at the rope he dropped to grab her. "I see you brought a grappling hook. Good. The wall is the only way in. I have studied the guards' movements. If you follow my direction and move when I say, we should be able to scale the wall before they notice."

The thud of hobnail-studded sandals marked the transit of another guard. They froze as one and held their breaths. The soldier clomped past. Grignr slung his tool bag over his shoulder and grabbed the rope. The seer caught his arm. She whispered, "Wait."

Heartbeats later, a second guard passed, marching in the opposite direction. She tucked the torches beneath her cloak. "Now," she ordered.

She jogged to a point in the wall some distance from the main gate, Grignr close behind. He hurled the hook. It scraped loudly over the whitewashed rocks. Finally, it caught. He tested it with a sharp tug.

"Hurry," she hissed.

An instant later he heard a garbled shout. He grabbed her by the waist and tossed her after the hook. She squealed in alarm but caught the rope and scrambled to the top of the wall. He whipped out his sword. The first guard was gutted before he finished the draw. He whirled to face the two guards now pounding at him from the other direction. Steel clashed on steel. The fighting men grunted, sweta flying from the gaps in their armor, gaps that moments later met Grignr's sword.

He'd just decapitated the final soldier when an angry shout drew his attention to the advance of two more. One plus two and two made five, he thought as his sword cleaved his nearest opponent's sword arm at the elbow. He screamed so loud, there was no need for the others to raise the alarm. The whole neighborhood must have heard. Grignr made quick work of the last soldier to face him. He was committed now. He scrambled up the wall.

Just as he was about to hoist himself over, seer's voice floated toward him. "Beware of the glass. You don't want to bleed here."

"It's too late for that."

He'd suffered no serious wounds in the fight, but there was sure to be blood, if only that of his opponents. Still, he took a moment to scan the top of the wall. Sharp glass teeth protruded from the plasteed stone, glinting hungrily in the moonlight. With a muttered curse, he adjusted his shifted his feet and sprang over the wall.

He landed lightly for such a large man. The cemetery was well-tended, its short-mown grass spongy underfoot. An errant thought of how easy it would be to dig upward from one of those neat, stone-marked graves skittered across his mind. He repressed a shudder.

The wench stood in front of four marble sarcophagi arrayed in a straight line in front of the cliff face, a lit torch in each hand. Her hood lay across her shoulders, exposing vines of orchid hair almost as pale as her skin. She frowned at his appearance and hissed, "I told you not to bleed."

"Well, you didn't tell the solders."

Her pout thinned. She presented him with one of torches. He lowered it, intending to extinguish it in the dirt.

"Stop that!" she snapped. "You must keep the flames between you and the tombs."

"The light will bring more soldiers," he grunted. "You should douse yours too. The moon can light our way."

"No soldier in Schist will venture here, day or night. Their orders are to kill any who seek entrance here and alert the prince of any attempt. We have nothing to fear from *them*."

With that, she turned. Hips jouncing under her lashing cloak, she stomped up the grassy aisle between the two middle toms to a double gate of glittering golden scrolls set into the hillside.

He started after her. The ground under his sandals sifted. He stumbled. Barbarian reflexes and muscular memories of the treacherous snows of his youth kept him upright, but he almost dropped the torch. The aisle between the bright sugar-white sepulchres rippled and bucked like something stirred beneath the sod.

"Stop that," the seer snarled. He didn't think she was talking to him. Her next words confirmed it. "You, Ecordian, circle around the tombs, and keep that torch between you and them!"

He met her at the gate. The golden loops that formed the barrier flashed reflected fire. A bar padlock ornamented with four misshapen skulls sealed the entrance. "Can you open it?" she inquired breathlessly.

Four skulls. Four tombs with something restless and troubling beneath them. One didn't need to be a scholar to see the implications. "What happens if I do?"

"We open the gates and enter the cave."

"And them?" He pointed his torch at the brooding sarcophagi.

"They will stay sealed so long as we keep the torches between ourselves and them. I will hold yours while you work."

After his experience of the restless ground and the prospect of facing something that might not be killable because it was already dead, Grignr wasn't sure he liked the ide of surrendering the torch. But having come this far, leaving without the jeweled sword was no longer an option. The escaped soldier would have his measure, and red-headed barbarians were rare this far south. He had no desire to tour the prince's prison or his galleys.

The seer stood behind him. He didn't like that either. He trusted her even less than he had before. But she kept the torches pointed at the graves. With a mental shrug, he pulled a crowbar from his backpack, shimmied it under the bar, and yanked. The lock dropped into his free hand. It was heavy but not weighty enough for gold. He cursed under his breath as he spread the loopy gates. The lunges screamed in protest, but there was only the dead to hear.

The seer returned his torch and entered the cave. He sidled after her, torch aimed outward, a small knife palmed in his free hand. On the way in, he scraped the blade against the frame of the gate. It met hard iron. The of the gates was nothing but gilt.

Sheathing the knife, he rubbed his chin. What did that portend for the fabled sword? He eyed the wench mistrustfully. She inserted the torch in a sconce beside the gate. The movement revealed a pale elegant calf rising to a dimpled knee and glowing thigh. On the other hand, someone had gone to great lengths to protect the contents of this cave. He settled his own torch in the matching sconce on the other side of the opening.

The walls of the cave rose like a stone tent to an acute point some yards above his head. The floor was bare and dusty except for a rune-covered boulder in the center of the room. The tangled incsriptions seem to wiggle in his sight. He dismissed it as the effect of flickering torchlight. He had no attention to spare for anything beyond the short length of sword protruding from the carved stone. The proportions of the hilt were odd. The pommel was the size and shape of a large pear, and the grip separating it from the guard would accommodate no more than two fingers of his hand. But he determined to make do. Flashing gems of every color and description protruded from the golden pommel and guard like the thick-packed cloves dotting a winter fair orange. The watered steel of the blade matched the silvery sheen of the diminutive grip. Their wavering patterns and the shimmer of the numberless jewels mesmerized him. Instinctively, he reached for the hilt.

"Wait!" she cried, catching his wrist in both of hers. "The sord is bound to the rock by dark magic. It cannot be withdrawn until I've broken the spell."

"How will you do that," he probed suspiciously.

"The counterspell is a prayer to Ousoon in the ancient tongue of our people. The prayer calls on him to release the lock, break the spell, and free the sword. Whatever you do, do not grasp the sword until the third time I call the holy name."

"Why? What will happen."

"I cannot say. But trust me, it will not be good."

That was the problem. He didn't trust her. His suspicions deepened as she began her chant. Strange sounds slithered from her lips. If ears could squint, perhaps he would have recognized some of the words, but the intonation grated, interspersed as they were with strange clicks and ratchets. The rhythm was as hypnotic as the shimmering blade. He found himself swaying with the measured phrases, his flared nostrils filled with the cloying whorehouse smell of sweat and orchids.

His mind reared up in protest. The wench wasn't unspelling the sword; she was enchanting him. A terrible roar erupted from the debts of his belly. He'd teach her to toy with an Ecordian!

He dropped his tool bag beside the rock, grasped the sword's upraised pommel, and pulled. The seer's chant ended in a shriek. In his daze, he could have sworn the sword pulled back. No, it was an illusion born of the stubby grip. The seer flew across the room, thowing herself against him to force him back. He batted her aside, knotting the fingers of both hands around the pommel, braced his sandals, and heaved.

An electric shock seared his hands. The bolt launched him backwards like a catapult. He landed on his rump and skidded toward the wall. He jumped to his feet and almost fell over. What had the witch done to him? He caught sight of his hands. The nails had turned the blue black of of a lightning strike. He bellowed in fury and reached for his own trusty sword. A tickle of hairy limbs crossed his sandaled foot. Spiders the size of his palm swarmed across the floor of the cave.

He hopped from foot to foot, expecting every second to be felled by some excruciatingly lethal venom. But the spiders weren't interested in him. The arachnid waves parted around him, rushing like the tide toward the seer backed against the far side of the stone chamber.

Somehow, she had retrieved one of the torches and was using its heat to drive the spiders back. "Fool," she hissed. "I told you not to draw the sword until I finished!"

"Then get on with it!"

"I'm a little busy right now!" she screeched, tearing off her cloak. She flung it into the spiders and set it alight.

She had a point. She was also naked but for the embroidered leather pouch tied to her waspish waist and a few scraps of sweat-stained silk.

Grignr blinked, then recalling himself to the situation, loped toward the remaining torch, his sandals kidding on the fat furry bodies coursing over the floor. He snatched up the brand. He still didn't trust her, but he had to save her. Mrifk would damn him to everlasting torment should he allow the defilement of such glorious pulchritude by the poison-spewing fangs of the carnivorous horde.

Besides, he needed her to release the jeweled sword.

Keeping the torch between him and the tombs beyond the gate, he swept the baton over spiders. Cinders flew from the spitting flames, igniting spiders wherever they fell. Unlike the flames from her cloak which receded as the patched fabric crisped and shriveled, the fire from his torch jumped from spider to spider. Their bodies exploded in a powdery ash, releasing a choking, putrid odor that sent bile roiling up his throat.

The seer screamed and dropped her flambeau. It guttered out. Her nearly naked body slumped against the wall. A dozen spiders spun their downy webs over her writing limbs, their mandibles clacking ominously.

"Barbarian!" she pleaded.

He raced to her side and plucked a pair of spiders from her perky breasts before they could jump to her eyes.

"You must burn them," she instructed. "Burn them all."

Before he could answer, the scrape of stone against stone whipped his head around. A hidden door in the back of the cave, indistinguishable from the wall around it, swung wide. Framed by the blackness of an underground tunnel, a squat, spindle-shanked rat of a man waved a smoking torch like a scepter. His flaccid lips pushed in and out in irate irritation. He shouted, "Prepare to die, thief!"

– 3 –

Grignr's brow crumpled in confusion. "Who are you?"

The overdressed interloper stamped his booted foot. "I am Cebaceous of Schist, prince of this land. What manner of scum are you that dares profanee the holiest shrine of my line and doesn't even know my name?"

"I am Grignr of Ecordia. Figt me, and it is you who shall die!"

The seer groaned. She kicked and tore at the webbing sealing her to the wall. But the busy spiders were faster than her hands.

Grignr caught his torch in his left hand and drew his sword. He circled right, not about to ignore the seer's warning now. Cackling, the prince unsheathed the sword on his right hip. Their swords met in a terrible clang. Cebaceous was no novice in the arts of wra. He fought with the speed and guile of a streetfighter, using his metal-sheathed torch as a veteran brawler used his knife. Grignr was taller, stronger, younger, and faster. But fighting a left-handed swordsman was always tricky, and he was hampered by his need to keep his Kalla-blessed torch between him and the nameless doom promised by the tombs.

Still, the youth's great reach stood him in good stead. His sword slashed across Cebaceous's pudgy chest, rending his gold-brocated tunic, squealing against the golden breastplate that lay beneath. Laughing, Cebaceous parried, pushing Grignr back. Steel crashed against steel. Stroke. Counterstroke. The cave sang with echoed clangor.

Dimly, through the red haze of battle and the noise of metal on metal, Grignr thought he heard the almost familiar sibilance of the seer's chant. Too sweet perfume filled his nostrils. His next blow knocked the torch from Cebaceous's hand.

Weaving his sword in Grignr's face, the prince retreated. The seer clacked her tongue and cried, "Ousoon!" She sounded like one in pain.

Grignr dodged his opponent's steel. He slammed his sword onto Cebaceous's left shoulder. The prince's shoulder dipped, but it didn't break. He didn't bleed. He didn't even drop his sword.

The toad-like prince laughed between pants. "None of my line can perish by the sword so long as Ounna's blade is trapped in the rockl. Now die!"

He rushed forward, propelled by a new burst of energy. The seer entreated, "Ousooon!"

Suddenly Grigner was on the defensive, retreating before the prince's harried blows. The Ecordian began to accept his sword was useless for anything except warding off Cebaceous's blows, which were flying too fast for strategy.

The seer howled, "Ousoon!" Death rattled in her throat.

Grignr slammed his sword against Cebaceous's head, the blade caught on his crown and shattered like cheap glass. But the blow served its purpose, causing Cebaceous to lower his guard. In the prince's moment of triumph, Grignr thrust the torch in his face. Cebaceous screeched as his hair, heavy with pomade, exploded into flame. He knocked his crown askew and tried to smother the flames with the rags of his finery. But their fight had shredded his clothes down to the armor beneath.

Tatters burn better than cloth. Grignr thrust his torch again and again at the fluttering rags. His relentless attack drove Cebaceous to the wall and kept him pinned until every scrap ignited, and the prince was a screaming column of fire. The torch sputtered and died.

A grinding sound, more distant but as loud as the noise that presaged the prince's presence, reverberated from outside. Grignr dropped the now useless torch and somersaulted to the center of the cave. This time, when he braced his feet and grasped the glimmering pear in both hands, the sword slid from the rock like a knife from butter.

A faint whimper recalled him to the girl on the other side of the room. Encased in webbing like a fly in some gargantuan spider's larder, she was in a piteous state. All he could see of her ravishing form was a small oval of face and the shrouded shape of the arm she had thrown up to shield her eyes. He reached for the knife strapped to his thigh, intending to cut her free.

"Use the sword, Grignr," she whined. "But gently. Gently!"

She didn't have to tell him twice. It was awkward maneuvering with his hand curled around the pear-shaped pommel instead of firmly grasping the hilt. But the cocooning webs parted at the merest kiss of the blade, sizzling into nothingness. The girl slumped to the floor, her magnificent chest heaving as if she had been the one to duel the sword-master prince, not he. A handful of bruises stood out against the pearly plushness of her flesh. A few unsmoked spiderwebs snarled the remains of her coiffure. Oddly, she seemed skinnier than he remembered, but otherwise unharmed.

The clatter outside increased. Her eyes flashed wide. "They're here!" she yodeld. "Cebaceous's torch, where is it?"

"By the rock," he advised as he whirled to face the gilded gates.

Moonlight illumed an unbelievable scene. Four long dead giants gathered at the head of their tombs. The desiccated remains of skin and sinew clinging to their bones were arrayed in rich armor, gleaming as if newly burnished by loving hands. Leathery skin bared skulls as well as teeth beneath their crested helms.

It was a waking nightmare. Superstitiious dread lifted the damp hairs at his nape. But he was Grignr, a barbarian unbowed, not some sniveling, city-bred guttersnipe. He clasped a magic sword (albeit one that was hard for a man of his stature to grasp) and now that he held it, a destiny.

He sprinted to the gate, closing the panels in the liches' faces, barring it with the bulging might of his shoulder. The revenant warriors crowded into the narrow opening. They jostled for position. Their metaled forms thudded against each other as they tried to force their way into a cut in the rock barely wide enough for one to pass. They clawed the gilded loops of the gate. Talon-like fingers raked his shoulder through the spaces between the scrolls.

Stabbing them through the gate had no effect. Grignr's blade slipped between bones or scraped rudely over their armaments. The moan of rancid air through their empty carcasses signaled another push forward. He leapt back.

The sudden release of the gate sent them toppling forward. The first dead giant splatted on the dusty floor at the Ecordian's feet. Grignr brought the sword down on his bared neckbones an instant before a second revenant fell atop the first. Grignr yanked his sword from between the revenants, almost overset by the awkwardness of his grip. Wielding the magic sword in battle was no easy matter.

The headless corpse of the first lich tried to rise as the remaining warriors marched into the cave. Some distance away, its decapitated skull clacked its rotten teeth. The head flipped from side to side as if the skull still lived and thought and was trying to roll its way back to Grignr.

Atavistic terror of the already dead fighting beyond yet another death spurred the barbarian to frenzy. His sword flew in sharp, cutting arcs that severed limbs. As they fell before him, he stomped on the disarticulated bones to crush them, but still the monsters advanced.

Then *she* was there, forcing them back with the torches as he had forced back the prince. What a woman! To fight light that after all she'd endured. Any Ecordian would be proud to call her his.

He fell upon the revenant warriors with renewed vigor. Only two remained a threat. One crawled forward on the stumps of shattered legs, and the other lacked an arm. Grignr brought his sword down hard, intending to shear through the legless giant's neck, but his uneasy grip fouled his strike. Instead of cutting through vertebrae, the blade struck the lich's cuirass. Steel locked on steel.

Groaning a ghastly moan of triumph, the giant reached for him, skeletal hands outstretched. Grignr released the pommel and stumbled back. The groping hands closed on empty air. But with his crowbar put away in his bag, he had only his knife to hand, while the other giant still had one good arm, one that ended in a hand gripping a massive sword.

The seer swept the prince's torch in front of the lich's face. He fell back. She thrust the torch into Grignr's empty hand. "Here."

She grasped the oddly shaped hilt of his immobilized sword, fingers knitting perfectly around the narrow grip. The blade slid free in a shriek of steel. The warrior uttered a gasp that was half moan and crumbled to ash as had the spiders before him. His empty armor clattered against the stone floor.

She turned to the remaining lich, her diminutive writs firm despite the weighty steel. She hefted the blade for the same stroke Grignr had bungled. She was the smallest, daintiest person in the cave, yet the blow smote her opponent like the hand of Mrfik, cleaving through steel, leather, and bone from shoulder to empty groin. There wasn't even time for the dead to scream. The bisected corpse thudded against the floor and disintegrated.

His torch immobilized the animate bones. In her hands, the sword vaporized them. But instead of helping Grignr finish the job, the girl strode purposefully toward the rune-ringed rock. Grignr shook his head, sure his eyes deceived him. The seer seemed to grow taller and thinner with every step. By the time she reached the boulder, the sword held in her upraised hands seemed to stretch halfway to the apex of the tall, pointed ceiling.

She brought it down like a hammer. The rock exploded in a thundercrack of light and slivered stone. The blast knocked Grignr off his feet. His head struck something hard, and the world went black.

- 3 ½ -

Cool blue light filtered through the groggy barbarian's eyelids. Was he dead? No. Too many things hurt, and when he reached up to touch his head, his fingers came away sticky. Opening his eyes took longer. The light was as bright as the hungry noontime sky over the Inland Desert, not shadowed like the light of his torch. The torch he no longer held.

His brow furrowed. How long had he been unconscious? If the sun had risen while he slept, he needed to flee. Someone would surely come to investigate, if only to discovered what had transpired with their prince, and he was in no condition to best them.

The realization of his sorry plight prompted his eyelids to part. At first, he didn't believe what his eyes revealed. He knuckled them, sure what he was seeing was a trick of the uncanny brightness. But when he opened them once more, the vision remained. He looked up at the incredible statuesque figure reaching almost to the ceiling of the cave. The glowing naked form resembled a woman, if one could imagine a woman who was half wasp, with hard, unnaturally round breasts topping an impossibly small waist and exaggerated ovular hips. The legs beneath must have been eight feet tall. The wasp woman held a proportionally long, jewel-handled ivory sword flat against her shoulder.

But strangest of all was her face. Beneath a tangled mane of vines studded with actual tiny orchids, enormous sapphirine eyes bulged from either side of a visage the color and texture of white orchid petels. Beneath those uncanny eyes, her face tapered to a sharp point. Her nostrils were no more than tiny slits above a tart, lipless mouth. If his gaze did not deceive him, the mouth smiled.

He lacked the strength to stand, but he pushed himself up on his elbows. After so many battles, he refused to meet his dom prone on his back.

"What are you?" he demanded harshly.

The narrow mouth widened, exposing not teeth but something that looked like a silver sparrow's bill. She replied, "I am Ounna, daughter of Ousoon, Mistress of Love and War."

She spoke with the seer's voice, but beneath the dulcet tones he heard the strange rattles and clicks he remembered from her counterspell. He rasped, "You deceived me!"

"I used you," she corrected. "For six generations, the people of Schist have been taught they will die if Ounna's sword was drawn from its stone. It was a lie, of course, promlegated to keep me bound to their princes' whim. But it ensured no child of Schist would come to my aid for fear killing all they held dear."

She hoisted the blade. From his lowly angle, he could clearly see her hand. It sported only two fingers and a curved, clawlike thumb that perfectly cupped the grip. She continued, "The dark mage who bound me also enchanted my sword. His mystic runes prevented me from touching it. Only a human could draw it from the rock and only with my help, which he and his line did everything in their power to deny."

"Then you found me. I set you free."

"Let us say you aided my efforts," she countered.

"Very well, I aided you," he concurred. "I know nothing about the southern gods, but where I come from, if a man does a favor for a god, he gains a favor in return."

She regarded him blandly. Whorls of glitter glistened over the front-facing facets of her bulging eyes. He tried to breathe normally. It was hard in the face of his racing heart and the hairs standing on the backs of his arms, but he refused to quail before her.

"My favor, little man, is I let you live."

She thrust her sword at the ceiling. As it pierced the peak, it simmered into insubstantiality. Her form became a translucent being of light. Gilded dust motes danced around the glow. Her shape grew thinner and straighter, then separated into flat planes of pallor angling upward. The planes became shafts arrowing toward the ceiling's apex. The stone drew them in like sand draws water in the desert.

The last of her light faded to nothingness, leaving him in darkness leavened only by the faintest gleam of moonlight reflected off the marble sarcophagi outside the gate. A terrible rumbling, like the loudest thunder, erupted overhead. He clapped his hands over his ears. The hill began to shake. He sat up, drew his knees to his chin, and despite her promise, prepared to enter the Halls of Mrifk.

- The not quite lost ending -

The tremors seemed to last forever. He must have passed out again, because the next time he opened his eyes, the cave was bright with daylight. He shuffled to the gilded gates on watery legs and peered outside.

The tombs fronting the gilded gates lay in ruins. The rest of the cemetery appeared undisturbed and deserted. The temples and businesses opposite, however, were alive with hubbub. He couldn't hear what the crowds were saying, but he saw no indication anyone was interested in what was happening beyond the cemetery's gates. If necessary, he could remain hidden until dark and scale wall between patrols.

If there were any patrols, he thought, remembering the earthquake that followed Ounna's disappearance. Either way, he could wait. The cave was cooler than the hot city streets and good place to recover his strength.

He turned back to the shadows and frowned. The crushed bones and dust which had littered the floor had vanished. Even the body of the prince had disappeared. Aside from the pervasive smell of scorched pig, all that was left were Cebaceous's sword, his jewels, the valuable antique armor of the dead, and Grignr's capacious tool bag.

"Well," the Ecordian chuckled. "Maybe her favor wasn't so bad after all."

Grignr and the Tomb of Really Bad Evil
Michael A. Ventrella

"Mrifk!" Grignr the barbarian snorted. "Truly, this tomb is really bad and evil."

His companions nodded. There was Azmi'flnrk, the elfin wizard carrying the Staff of Lobert, Ilandria the cleric that healed when needed and of course Grignr's true love Carthena who sadly did not always return Grignr's feelings but still tempted him with her lush udders and stuff and whose skill with puzzles and arcane locks had made her a good thief Grignr had to admit.

"It is indeed and one can feel it truly," said Azmi'flnrk. "The tomb opens with a secret word but I cannot read these runes to say what that word could be."

"Words!" Grignr ejaculated. "Grignr needs not words!" He hefted his mighty club, won from the dwarven mines in Grunthor, and smashed the door, which responded by doing nothing. Grignr smashed and smashed as his companions waited. Finally, tired and exhausted and drained and pooped, Grignr sat. "The slut must be made of magic!" he said.

"You keep using that word…" Ilandria said, but Carthena stepped forward, pulling out her lockpicking tools and without a word, lockpicking the lock and opening the door.

"Simple," she said, looking straight at Grignr.

The dusty door creaked open, revealing a dark passageway to where the treasures of the tomb surely lay, awaiting the adventurers.

"This is where the treasures of the tomb surely lay, awaiting us adventurers," said Azmi'flnrk, waving his hand over the Staff of Lobert and causing a bluish light to emit. He turned to Grignr. "You first."

Grignr nodded. He knew that as the strongest and bravest and fastest and strongest, he should always go first, but just as he began, a cry came from the tomb, and a group of skeletons carrying rusty swords and polearms and battleaxes and halberds and one with just a shield it found lying around one afternoon came rushing forward.

"Wandering monsters!" screamed Azmi'flnrk.

"No, they're in a dungeon so they aren't wandering," Carthena replied bustily.

"Now is not Argument Time!" Grignr screamed. "Now is Kill The Evil Skeletons What Live in the Evil Dungeon and Have Big Weapons Time!" He bounded toward the boney creatures, hacking and slaying as clavicles, humeruses, femurs, coccyxes, metatarsals, tibias, patellas, skulls, and especially hyoid bones bounced around the halls, careening off all surfaces even the ceiling but not that much off the ceiling. Within a few seconds, all was silent.

"No fair," Ilandria said. "You didn't give us a chance and now you get all the experience."

"Experience is what makes me great!" said the enthused Ecordian, as he strode into the dungeon, squinting through the dim light brought by the wizard.

"Look, ahead!" Azmi'flnrk said. And, indeed, as they processed down the path of evil, lit braziers on the walls made vision easier. "Someone is here because why would these be lit otherwise?"

"I thought you said this was an abandoned tomb from the Era of Darkness," Ilandria said.

Azmi'flnrk pouted. "Well yes, that's what the guy who sold us this map said."

"Grignr will punish the evil that lights torches in abandoned tombs from the Era of Darkness!" the crusty barbarian ejaculated loudly. He marched forward, his nimble orbs darting toward danger. From behind him, he could hear the sighs as his adventuring companions followed.

As he reached the lit torches, Grignr stopped. The floor ahead was covered with strange runes. "Mrifk!" he cursed. "I cannot read these arcane symbols!"

Azmi'flnrk slowly made his way forward and, leering around the husky man in a loincloth, peered around and looked around. Looking around, he saw the writing on the floor. "It's just standard letters in the common language, which makes no sense if this is an ancient tomb existing before the—"

"I am not afraid of letters!" Grignr shouted as he stepped forward.

"No!" everyone else shouted, but the enthused barbarian plodded ahead, stepping on letter after letter. A bluish-whitish-greenish-pinkish crimson gas seeped into the room from unseen locations.

"Step back!" Azmi'flnrk yelled, and the three companions backed up, away from the gas. "It's feeblemind gas! It will destroy your brain!"

Grignr continued his walk and reached the end of the hall and examined the door before him. "Door!" he yelled to his fellow adventurers, seen dimly in the light in the distance. "It looks closed."

The gas had dissipated and Azmi'flnrk motioned to everyone that it was now safe to pass.

"I thought you said the gas would destroy our brains," Carthena said, indicating Grignr.

Azmi'flnrk shrugged. "No brains, no effect."

The door was large and big, with ornate fanciness covering the side facing the adventurers who didn't know what the other side looked like.

Carthena stepped forward. "I'll check for traps," she said, checking for traps. Convinced there were none, she stepped backwards and waved her arm to indicate that there were no traps.

Wasting no time, Grignr flung the door open and dashed into the room. The room was 30 by 30 with a small lozenge-shaped alcove containing a raised platform. Torches cast dancing shadows on the adventurers. Tapestries of ancient sacrifices decorated the walls except one wall that had a blank spot where a tapestry had been removed. On the raised platform was a throne made of the finest ivory which looked very uncomfortable to sit in, but even so, sitting in it was a skeletal figure wearing a crown covered in jewels and stuff that didn't look uncomfortable at all. The skeletal figure, not the crown.

"The missing tapestry means something," Ilandria mused, stroking her chin like a person who muses does.

Grignr growled. "Foul creature, you do not deserve to live!" he yelled, holding up his sword, pointing toward the throne. "Justice will be served!"

"Seriously?" the creature said. "You break into my home, and attack me, and *I'm* the bad guy?"

Grignr paused. Was this some sort of parlay he did not understand?

"Great lich," said Azmi'flnrk. "We are humbly here to—you are a lich, are you not? I just assumed with the crown and everything—"

"Yes, yes," the lich replied. "That's me, and you have no chance of defeating me and I shall turn you all into my skeletal minions like I have every other adventurer who has come here, so you might as well surrender now and make everything easier."

"Ah," Azmi'flnrk replied. "Yes. Well." He nodded to his companions and quietly said, "There is no way we can defeat a lich. He's much too powerful."

"Can he be turned?" asked the cleric.

"No," the lich replied, standing and waving his skeletal arm toward everyone. "I am way too powerful and immune to anything you can throw at me. And I can hear perfectly well. I know, you wouldn't think so, with me having no obvious ears and all, but then again, here I am speaking without lips or lungs so go figure."

"But what do you want?" Azmi'flnrk asked. "Why are you here? And what happened to the tapestry that's missing?"

"Why am I here? Why, it's the perfect place to gain treasure and minions. It's easy, really—I control some idiot to go into taverns and sell maps to the place and then kill all the adventurers who come here and then I take their loot. It's quite a profitable enterprise, really. I can sell what I don't need and that helps finance the place. The upkeep is ridiculous, as you can imagine. As for the tapestry, that caught fire last week when Larry moved a flame too close to it while moving the tables around for our annual conference. I've ordered a replacement, but it won't be delivered until Thursday."

"This is too much talk!" Grignr said.

"Indeed," the lich said. "So I'll just kill you all now." The lich raised its staff, which started glowing menacingly in crimson shades of crimson. His eye sockets began to glow and he raised his arms menacingly. "You should all be very afraid."

"Grignr fears nothing!" the barbarian yelled.

"Wait, what? Did you say 'Grignr'?" The lich took a step backwards.

Grignr bounded forward, sword hacking before him. The lich jumped off the pedestal and began wildly swinging his staff, but didn't get far before Grignr hacked into him.

"Not fair!" the lich shouted as he ran around the room, pursued by the crazed barbarian.

Grignr, unable to match the magical speed of the undead thing, took a short cut and bounded onto the pedestal. He grabbed the chair the lich had been sitting in and with his massive muscles bulging, picked it up and tossed it at the lich. It smashed into it and the lich shattered into pieces, its magic dissipating before him.

"I don't believe it!" Azmi'flnrk said.

"Yes," Grignr said, beaming with pride. "Grignr is an expert with throne weapons."

"No, you idiot, you did it again! You grabbed all the experience for yourself."

Grignr sat down, confused. Why were his companions not happy? He closed his eyes and prayed to the gods, but the gods were laughing at him. He could tell. He felt that he could see them, sitting around a table, eating thinly sliced, heavily-salted potatoes and drinking some sort of sickly sweet brown ale. They appeared to be playing dice with his existence.

He stood. "Mrifk!" he said. "I will never understand the ways of you adventurers."

Carthena puffed out her ample bosom and sighed. "It's fine, Grignr. No one expects you to understand anything."

Grignr nodded happily, knowing that Carthena would do the thinking for him, leaving him free to be the bravest, strongest, daringest, courageousest, spunky, hero-like hero barbarian ever to be a heroic barbarian ever.

About the Authors

KEITH R.A. DeCANDIDO first participated in an *Eye of Argon* reading sometime in the 1990s. He has won the competition on several occasions, managing to last longer than anyone else participating. He has also read it while doing various voices, among them Kermit the Frog and Todd Rage, a character he voiced on the *HG World* audio drama. When he isn't reading *Eye of Argon*, which is, to be fair, most of the time, he writes fiction in novel, short story, and comic book form and pop culture commentary for various sources both print and online. Find out less at his web site at http://www.DeCandido.net.

GENEVIEVE ISEULT ELDREDGE (she/they) discovered their first *Eye of Argon* reading while late-night wandering the halls at PhilCon, and since being sucked in, has read for Grignr, the rat, and both Grignr and the rat simultaneously. She's also read while doing impressions of Chiana and Sikozu from *Farscape* and at least once as Chewbacca. When she isn't pretending to be a fiery-haired barbarian, GIE writes angsty, slow-burn lesbian stories about girls who can't decide whether to kiss or kill each other. Sometimes they do both. Learn more about GIE and her disaster lesbians at https://www.girlyengine.com/

DANIEL M. KIMMEL is the 2018 recipient of the Skylark Award, given by the New England Science Fiction Association. He was a finalist for a Hugo Award for *Jar Jar Binks Must Die... and Other Observations About Science Fiction Movies* and for the Compton Crook Award for best first novel for *Shh! It's a Secret: a novel about Aliens, Hollywood, and the Bartender's Guide*. In addition to short stories, he is the author of *Time on My Hands: My Misadventures in Time Travel*, *Father of the Bride of Frankenstein* and (with Deborah Cutler-Hand) *Banned in Boston*. He is also a working film critic (http://www.NorthShoreMovies.net) and writes the "Take Two on the Movies" column for *Space and Time* magazine, spotlighting classic (and not so classic) SF films.

MONICA MARIER is a caffeinated writer, artist, mother, and eccentric. On weekdays, she's a co-founder of Tangent Artists, a webcomic company where she writes and does art for three comics series. She is also a co-author of the popular *Handbook for Saucy Bard* series. She fervently hopes for an eighth day of the week to be instated so she can sleep. Monica currently resides in Northern Virginia with her husband and two kids. She is often seen walking down the sidewalks of Historic Warrenton, muttering character dialogue to herself. Her web page is https://monicamarier.com/.

PRETER PRELLWITZ bean righing stories, plays and skits? since the 5fth grade. As a child kid and young peeple persin, Peter glorificlly visioned limited publication of one play and two seriouss of chidldern's puppet skis. Hooking his bloddy pumping heart for life on the heartfeelt of exclamatory worthy jorny of rithgting. Presently atthe presetn momentum! Peyer has twelfth many novels he rote with words pubished in tralde paperback and E!ebook and trde papbak, now with AYE OF ARGON, He is! Top of his frantastic creer and feels outstaniding astoundedness of joy. (By the way, what's the title? *"Nose of Argon: We Hit It Between The Eye"*?)

HILDY SILVERMAN has been performing *The Eye of Argon* as horribly as possible for more than a decade at a variety of SF conventions. She particularly enjoys rolling like a tub of upset jelly. When she isn't hamming it up with her fellow author/performers, she writes and edits fiction in various genres, with her work appearing in numerous themed anthologies. For more information, please visit her website, http://www.hildysilverman.com.

IAN RANDAL STROCK plays with words for money. He thinks of himself as a science fiction writer, even though 98% of his published words have been non-fiction. He's worked in commercial space, on Wall Street, as a teacher, and as a tour guide, though he keeps stumbling back into the publishing world, where he currently edits, publishes, designs, markets, does the accounting for, and frets about Fantastic Books. His current worry is publishing this book; he's not sure if he should regret it, or simply remove his and the company's name from it. Tune in to http://www.FantasticBooks.biz to see what he decides to do. And if you're really curious about him (really? are you sure?) check out his personal web site at http://www.IanRandalStrock.com, or just go surfing the social media (his name is unique on the internet). He's also a really big fan of chapters 3½ and 7½; not for their content, just for the numbering.

JAMES F. THEIS was born August 9, 1953 and died March 26, 2002. He published "The Eye of Argon" in a fanzine in 1970 at age 16. He did not write any more fiction, but did earn a degree in journalism. His hobbies included collecting books, comics, and German swords; he also collected, traded, and sold tapes of radio programs of the 1930s, '40s, and '50s under the business-name "The Phantom of Radio Past," advertising in such publications as the *Fandom Directory*.

MICHAEL A. VENTRELLA writes humorous novels like *Bloodsuckers: A Vampire Runs for President*, *Big Stick*, and the *Terin Ostler* fantasy series. He has edited a dozen anthologies, including *Release the Virgins*, *Three Time Travelers Walk Into…*, *Across the Universe* (with co-editor Randee Dawn) and the *Baker Street Irregulars* series (with co-editor Jonathan Maberry). His own stories have appeared in other anthologies, including the *Heroes in Hell* series, *Rum and Runestones*, and *The Ministry of Peculiar Occurrences Archives*. His web page is http://www.MichaelAVentrella.com

JEAN MARIE WARD discovered sword and sorcery in college while attempting to convince a passing demon to type her homework. Rudely ejected into the working world, she eked out an uncertain existence scribbling fiction, nonfiction, and a bunch of government stuff she can't about. (No, really. People get *upset*.) But all good things come to an end. *The Eye of Argon* pulled her into its eldritch orbit, damning her to an eternity of mangled pronunciation and discontinuous plot points. Between heroically bad readings of Grignr's adventures, she is a frequent contributor to *Galaxy's Edge* magazine; Con-Tinual, the convention that never ends; passing anthologies; and Falstaff Books. Learn more at http://www.JeanMarieWard.com